Strange Sands Suspense 3
Charleston

The Freedom Staircase

Pamela Poole

Southern Sky Publishing

Cover picture is created with help from Craiyon tools online
Cover created on BookBrush
Ebook ISBN: 9781956089301
Print ISBN: 9781956089318
Print ISBN: 9781956089325

Author's Note

Have you ever walked into a place and instantly became ill at ease? Did you ever meet a person and your spirit clashed with his or hers? Was there ever a time when you couldn't explain it, but you simply knew something bad might happen at any moment—and it did?

The novellas in the Strange Sands Suspense series will follow the adventures of a young lady named Mercedes Ellison, whose family has a long history of unexplainable encounters. But then, Christians are peculiar people who should live supernatural lives.

The stories and people in this series are fictional, but they are inspired by places I've been, situations I've experienced, and people I interviewed who have had these encounters—encounters they typically keep to themselves. Each story will contain at least one event from my interviews, and sometimes several. If you'd like to know more about seeing the supernatural through the lens of a Christian worldview, check out the **Resources** list I suggest at the end of the book. If you are part of a Christian book club, you might appreciate the **Discussion Topics** page.

I hope you'll enjoy the Southern Lowcountry ambiance depicted in this series, where moments spent on warm sandy beaches blend with faith and the grains of slipping sand in history's hourglass.

Chapter 1

The Spirit-filled life is not a special, deluxe edition of Christianity. It is part and parcel of the total plan of God for His people.
-A. W. Tozer

Mercedes was excited about working with clients to evaluate a plantation mansion with a feature called the Freedom Staircase, and she was in no mood to debate the Patriot cause in the American Revolution with a guy who was half British. In her opinion, her boyfriend had a serious gap in his history education and needed to take another look now that he lived in the Lowcountry of South Carolina, home of the Swamp Fox and four signers of the Declaration of Independence.

She rubbed the tension over her brows. "I don't want to argue, Quincy. Frankly, I doubt you could understand this. You may have been born here in America, but you spent your life mainly with the British side of your family and traveling the world to archaeology sites. Strong opinions about patriotism come from the heart more than the head. Let's just agree to disagree."

Quincy jerked back his head to cushions on the pale gray leather sofa and looked heavenward, as if praying for patience. "If this issue is so dear to your heart, Mercedes, I want to understand it in my head. The people called 'rebels' as patriots in the Revolution were divided less than one hundred years later, insulting citizens as being 'rebels' who supported

Southern independence and state sovereignty. Families and friends became mortal enemies."

Mercedes huffed. "Now you're going into another era, and wow, that's an interesting accusation, since Great Britain's history is packed with wars in which families and friends became treacherous enemies and royalty killed family members to keep power and a throne. Maybe the colonists got used to that from living in England?"

She rose from her seat beside him. "My patriotic interest in this job is the American Revolution, the Patriots, Sons of Liberty, Whigs, and, yes, rebels. They wanted the Loyalists, Royalists, Tories, and King's Friends—anyone loyal to the British—to remain here as a valuable part of society. Like the Civil War, less than one hundred years later, yes, families got torn apart. I'm going back to work now."

He quickly reached for her hand. "I'm sorry our lunch break turned into this debate, and it's my fault. Please, sit back down."

With a sigh, Mercedes perched on the edge of the sofa. He gently tugged her arm, pulling her closer to him. "I'll look into this and fill in that gap in my education, okay? You're right, I spent little time in American history other than events and dates, and I focused on ancient things, studying whatever I needed wherever I was in the world. It's high time I learned about my country."

She nodded. He tried to keep the pleading tone out of his voice. "I don't need a desk and extra screen this afternoon. Let's take our laptops out to the Carolina room and work by the river view."

Mercedes was moody, withdrawn, and distracted. Quincy watched her out of the corner of his eye as she sat nearby in an ample white wicker chair with her bare feet on the wide, matching stool. She rested against fabric cushions printed with palm fronds in tropical shades of blue. If he was a painter, he would ask her to pose like this.

But her mind was back in the 1700s, he could tell. Ever since she started working on the plantation mansion job yesterday, she was somewhere else—and he was jealous. He did not understand her distraction. In his frustration, he had picked a fight with her. It was stupid on his part. He knew better than to demean the importance of America's founding and the role of heroes from the Lowcountry. She would drop a guy for less than that. The words were out of his mouth before he used his brain, and it would be no easy feat to regain her esteem.

He followed her up to Charleston for this job, unwilling to stay in his carriage house summer rental without her being two doors down in a cottage. She was planning to stay here with her family for a week and drive up to the plantation when needed. His family had not settled in their Charleston property, and he accepted the invitation to stay in the Ellison's guest cottage while she was home. It was a chance to engage his ulterior motive of spending time with her brother and parents again, talking to them about his plans for the future, and a welcome way to be with her without the restrictions of living in separate places in Bluffton.

The idyllic plans he had of getting closer to her were now mere castles in the air. He was not important enough to sidetrack her from wherever she went in her mind and heart with that plantation. If he wanted to be on her radar, he needed to do some research or be an attentive student when she shared her work.

He opted for the tactic of being a student. "Since Majestic Oaks is rich in history, why are the owners not trying to make it a state park or museum?"

Mercedes looked up from her laptop screen, and he waited as her eyes cleared from wherever she had been in her mind. She stretched one pretty foot on the wicker stool, pointing and flexing her blue pedicured toes. "They need to sell before the long process of fundraising and clearing red tape, but they hope to find a buyer who will keep it working instead of selling off the land. So far, the state is only interested in the house and immediate grounds. The family wants as much of the property as possible to remain with the house. They have sold chunks of it over the years, so it's a fraction of what it was when it was built as a rice plantation."

"Someone's been living there?"

She shifted her laptop computer and glanced over at him. "Yes, most of the time. It was being rented out by the last owner, a great-uncle who was in declining health and had to go live with one of my clients for the past year. The tenants were friends of the family, staying on as a favor for the owner, though they did well, cultivating the landscaping nurseries and other agriculture on the property and maintaining the old mansion. They could lease those portions out to entrepreneurs who don't have deep pockets. The property is by a river, so there are resources to manage. But the current renters are aging and ready to retire, so it works out for all concerned to sell."

Quincy raised a dark brow. "Have there been any historical dig sites on the grounds?"

Mercedes grinned at his archaeological curiosity. "Not enough, and if you're interested, we could ask about investigating. They have occasional educational tours and some college groups out, but they all seem focused on the environment, not on preserving history. Some metal detector clubs have gotten permission to search a few areas around the old slave quarters. Not all plantations were cruel places and many of the slaves at Majestic Oaks stayed there after emancipation in the Civil War. The master of the house went off to the battlefields, and the loyal, long-time slaves tried to protect the big house from possible plundering by Union soldiers. They took furnishings in boats down the river, and they returned many after the war. I'll see those when I go out there tomorrow. But according to family records, in the confusion, the family silver and some other valuables never were found. Ever since, owners tried digging up the most likely spots to search for these heirlooms, but maybe they failed because these were the likely locations. There is no written record of all the generals and troops who came through, though some were in the area."

He shifted in his chair. "Was anything found by the metal detector club?"

"Oh, yes. Coins, interesting buttons, and so on. A few of the families stayed on for generations, and the owners called them guardian angels of the plantation and best friends they grew up with. Some were so well respected by both the owners and workers that they became valuable foremen."

"If you can get permission, I'd like to go out with some equipment and a map of the property. Any cemeteries?"

She nodded. "You bet. They dedicated one to the slaves and workers who lived there, so the people who didn't choose burial at their church cemeteries had a place on the plantation. They liked to be laid to rest by water, so this one is above what used to be the spring flood boundaries. Of course, that's a consideration in the property's sale and the cemetery has its own road for families to access it. The family has maintained it over the years, so the surrounding forest hasn't taken over."

"If I clear my schedule, do you mind if I ride up with you to the Oaks? Unless having a tag-along will make you look unprofessional."

Mercedes studied him suspiciously. "Of course, you can come along. I'm only meeting with one client, and he inherited the largest portion of the estate. His two cousins aren't in town. Wallace is laid-back and genuine to talk to. Why are you suddenly interested in the plantation?"

He shrugged. "I've always learned history better hands-on."

Wallace Hampton snorted and kicked a pinecone the size of his fist out of the driveway. "The way the government spends my tax money is an immoral disaster. They won't do any better managing my family plantation. If it weren't for my cousins, I'd make this work instead of selling out, but I understand their reasons. One says her special-needs grandbaby needs a surgery that insurance won't cover, and the other cousin says he has become disabled. Both need the money for out-of-control medical bills. They've never lived here, never even visited, and I never met them. Their families married off a couple generations ago and didn't return. I appreciate Mary takin' my uncle in the last year, though. That's why she got a portion."

He shook his head and heaved a deep sigh. "It ain't no secret I got the mansion and the biggest share in the plantation by far, and I'd move back up here in a minute and take over. But I can't pay them off their part. I'm stuck between a rock and a hard place, and this truly breaks my heart."

Mercedes said, "I gathered this from our emails. Thanks for agreeing to meet me here without the real estate agent, so you can share your feelings about it and fill me in on all the things I'd miss behind the scenes. You said the agent is urging you to consider some aggressive buyers who are offering much less than the value. Does she think your appraiser is wrong, or is she expecting the property will be on the market for a long time?"

Hampton shook his head again and scowled. "I'll be honest, Miss Ellison, I don't know. The lawyer recommended the agency she's with, and when my cousin called, this is the agent they said had room in her schedule for handling an estate like ours."

"Mr. Hampton, if you can give me the name and contact information of the agent, I'd like to do some research to be sure she has experience in handling this kind of property. I have friends in real estate, and they're swamped right now, so her agency may be overwhelmed and forced to put her into the field. Don't sign a contract unless you are confident you have the right agent. Selling a condo near the beach is nothing like selling a historic site."

"Yes, ma'am, I'd appreciate that. It crossed my mind, but I haven't had time to check on it. And just call me Wallace."

She smiled. "Okay, Wallace. I like to be on a first name basis. I'm Mercedes, and this is Quincy."

Wallace nodded at Quincy. "Mercedes told me you're an archaeologist. You're welcome to poke around here, as long as you aren't alone. There are a lot of ways to get lost and hurt on the property. I have a guy who's worked around here for years, and if I can't be with you, he would be a great guide. Find some treasure so I can sell it and keep this place."

"I hope to do that if we can work it out. I have a flexible schedule."

"And I'm runnin' out of time to raise some money," Wallace said grimly. "Let's go look at the house, then I'll show you around the grounds."

Mercedes listened intently and made notes on her tablet as she and Quincy followed Wallace Hampton around. With a grand wave at the area to the front of the house, he pointed out that though there were two good roads to use as driveways, they should always use the second one they came to. The first led to a barn and public parking area for the landscaping nurseries and other services. "You followed my directions well today. Just remember to wait until you get to an avenue of old oaks, and it will be the private driveway to the front of the house. There's a path and you can get to the back porches from the other parking area, as well as the nurseries and cemetery. When the river was the main road, the back of the house was the front. They added this grand portico in 1790, in time for George

Washington's tour of the Lowcountry, creating a new front entrance."

He led them through a tall flowering hedge along a flagstone and shell walk from the drive to the front portico of a Georgian-style mansion. Beside her, she heard Quincy catch his breath. Eight white, elegant columns stood as they had for over two centuries, impressive in their simple dignity. They were two stories high, three on each side of wide marble stairs and one on each end of the deep front portico. Arched brickwork created openings for basements and cellars in the raised foundation.

Wallace spoke like a tour guide accustomed to showing the property to visitors. "In the winter, these camellia japonicas will bloom in a riot of color, giving the mansion a festive air for the holidays. The only place around here with more varieties of camellias is Magnolia Gardens." He pointed in the direction where the other parking area must be if they could see it. "People come from all around to get some new bushes grown from ours in our nurseries when we have them. They get our oaks, flowering trees, and other landscaping plants."

Through gardens that led to the front of the mansion, Wallace showed them unusual botanical specimens and sunny, tropical shrubberies that grew well in the soil and climate. "These garden benches, freed people who chose to stay here made 'em. See that ironwork, with all the winding vines and leaves? There are no more made like this design around Charleston, even by Simmons."

Quincy's cellphone vibrated and he checked to see if it was urgent. It was.

"I'm sorry, this isn't a call I can ignore," he said. "You two go ahead, I'll catch up in a few minutes."

He stepped into the shade of a massive oak with an old bell suspended on an iron bar between two split trunks. He touched his phone screen to call the officer he contracted with for an antiquities fraud investigation that ended with the capture of the Lenoir Bassett and Madigan law firm. The investigation and arrests happened a month ago, and the officer said he had news about the case.

"I'll send you something official tomorrow, but I knew you had a reason to want to hear about this before you watch it on the news. Stanley Lenoir was found dead in his jail cell this morning. Apparent suicide, but no one has any straight answers that satisfy me yet. I don't know what other contracts you've got in the works right now, but considering the threats his son made recently, you should stick close to Miss Ellison. I'm getting some hints around here that she and Zach Boone may be encouraged to go into protective custody."

"What?" Quincy exclaimed. He glanced to the stately front portico, but Mercedes had moved indoors with her client. "I'm with her right now, on a job. Her job." He sighed and looked around the expanse of the front lawn and gardens of the plantation. "Look, I've got no other pressing obligations right now except consulting on a dig in St. Augustine. I'll stay close to Mercedes. What about Jana and Declan, friends she was with in Hilton Head that night of the arrests?"

"There have been no more threats against them coming my way, but I'll get an update. I'll send Roland Lenoir's photo so you can keep an eye open. You're back on this job, Quincy, working for us. We've had reason to monitor Roland ever since we started connecting his dad to criminal activity, of which the fraud we snagged him on was only a drop in the bucket. His son has some contacts in low places, and he has insider access to knowing Mercedes' and Zach's movements. If you two can arrange an invitation for her friends to visit, all the better."

Quincy pinched his forehead. "Straight up—are you free to tell me if spooks or assassins silenced Stanley Lenoir, and what country they represent? His involvement in the antiquities black market and other nefarious circles went deep and worldwide. You promised I worked far enough away from this situation not to be considered a threat to those circles."

The man sighed. "I'm not free to confirm or deny the country of origin of the suspects being considered for pulling off this feat, but I don't need to comment on their skill level for you to comprehend it. My first instinct is to assure you there's no danger of any group thinking you know too much. You should be in no danger and therefore bring none to Miss Ellison. However, I said Lenoir was secure where we put him, so I'm not as smug today and don't blame you for doubting me. His son could be the next target, so they may take him out, ending his threat to Miss Ellison and Mr. Boone. We haven't been able to get our hands on several things we wanted, and we believe Lenoir set up a message system to his son to get those in the event of his arrest or death."

Turning to scrutinize his surroundings, Quincy bit his lip. He knew he was better off not knowing anything specific. "Okay, uh—I'll start working to watch over Mercedes on this end. Is there any reason I can't do a little treasure hunting here for her client? I can keep her busy and away from home during the day."

"I'll run a location on your phone to see where you are. Give me a few facts about the job there. If this situation becomes more dangerous, we'll put someone on duty watching the family residence in Charleston. Carry your gun."

Washington Oak at Hampton Plantation

By Pamela Poole

I did this painting in a pastel workshop with famed artist Albert Handell. It's based on my photograph after visiting Hampton Plantation near Charleston, SC. Hampton is the primary inspiration for the property used in this story. George Washington visited Hampton Plantation in 1791, and the story goes that when asked whether they should let a young live oak grow where it had sprung up in view of the front door, he said yes. It is there to this day.

Patriot fighters like Francis Marion, the Swamp Fox, and his men used Hampton as a safe house to pass through. One account says he escaped Tarleton's arrival at the mansion by using the secret passage and fleeing to the river.

Chapter 2

Quincy let himself in the mansion through the front doors, marveling at the massive lockset on them and wondering what size the key was. An air-conditioned foyer welcomed him, and he nodded at a housekeeper who was dusting. She smiled and pointed to the right, and he stepped through to something like a sitting room or reception area for hosting guests. Antique furnishings made it look like a movie set for a nineteenth century historic drama, and he stopped in his tracks when he noticed what appeared to be Delft tile around the fireplace.

Muttering an exclamation of surprise, he stepped close enough to examine the scenes painted in blue and white. Many represented Bible stories, such as the nativity for the birth of Christ. He squatted and reached out reverently to touch it, then noticed one depicting David and Goliath.

It was only when he heard Mercedes' voice in the distance that he withdrew his hand and reluctantly rose to his feet again. He walked into the next room, where an enormous ballroom stretched from the front of the house to the back. He gaped at the decorative panels on the walls and the two-story vaulted ceiling painted in sky blue.

Mercedes smiled and walked toward him. "Wallace was just telling me there were once two large mirrors hanging in here, in mahogany frames painted white and imported from France in the nineteenth century. They were a wedding gift for a noblewoman, a French bride in the family lineage, and are among the missing furnishings after the Civil War. And they cut these boards on the floor from yellow pine grown here on the plantation."

Quincy scanned the expanse of the room. "They must be forty feet long!"

Wallace beamed with pride. "Every bit of it. We still grow these pines on the property. Yellow pine is so flinty and durable that even termites give up on it. This house is built of brick, marble, granite, yellow pine, and black cypress, that's why it has survived so many years. It may be out of style, but it endured."

He pointed to a fireplace seven feet wide. "See how the hearth of this fireplace sits up about half an inch? That's the only thing badly affected by the big earthquake back in 1886, and we left it as a part of history. Not much else got damaged that we've found, but there's a crack from after the quake in the foundation in the cellar."

The fireplace had the same tiles as the one in the sitting room, and Quincy took quick steps over to examine it. "This tile," he said. "Do you know anything about it?"

Wallace came closer. "They're mentioned in an inventory taken of the house contents after the Revolution, when the British considered the owner a traitor and plundered the property. They made a note under that line on the inventory that there were more tiles to match them in crates, probably for future improvements to the house. But I've looked in closets and the attic and can't find them anywhere. Supposed to be antique before they built the house in 1740 and shipped from Europe in other building materials and furnishings."

"You bet they're antique! If I'm on target, these are mid-1600s, and if you have more, they're valuable."

"No kidding? Maybe you can help me find where they're stored or hidden away."

Wallace gave them a tour of the rest of the house, which included features to accommodate guests. "Hospitality was almost a religion here in the South," Mercedes told Quincy. "Plantation owners greeted and welcomed travelers and strangers. The owners had the reputation of being generous-hearted and for not making social spectacles of themselves. One European visitor's journal about his travels said the women here in the Lowcountry drank water and the men were sober and industrious. He wrote about how refined plantation life was and how it lacked the vulgarity of city life."

"Oh, yes," Wallace said. "Even after we moved the kitchen indoors in modern times, tradition dictated that we have an 'unexpected guest' pantry. You'd get your hand slapped for reaching into it for anything, and that's where the best stuff was. There were years when visitors came to Majestic Oaks about every other day, and you never knew when relatives might show up to spend a month."

On the way down the handsome staircase, Wallace told them about the legends of the patriots who showed up at the house and how they always connected with the stairs. "My uncle and I never figured it out, but my grandparents and great-grandparents knew the secret of the 'Freedom Staircase.'"

As they reached the landing on the first floor and turned, he took them down a hallway and pushed the wallpaper. A door where there was none opened into a dark, musty passageway. Wallace coughed, then said, "We'll explore that another day."

"I'm impressed," Quincy said as he drove out of the Majestic Oaks main driveway. "And when we come back tomorrow, we'll need the jeep."

Mercedes laughed. "Right. No dirty shovels and boots in this sparkling new convertible."

He grinned. "I bought this with you in mind, honey! A beautiful carriage for my beautiful lady. Guess I need a truck, though, since my equipment won't fit in here."

She pointed to the right at an intersection for him to follow on a sandy road through woods. "We'll need to pack food and water for a long day. A change of clothes, a laptop, camera, portable chargers. The mansion is open to us, as well as the landscaping nursery facilities."

Quincy nodded as she guided him through another change in direction to get to the main highway. "This is a seat-of-my-pants treasure hunt, not a dig site, so I don't have many resources. I'll do some aerial reconnaissance, maybe get a friend to help me with satellite analysis of the property. I packed my drone in the stuff being moved to my parent's house in Charleston."

"My brother has one that might work out, and we have a canopy tent in case we need shelter from the sun or rain. The summer heat can be brutal here."

He reached over for a quick squeeze of her hand. "We've been in heat worse than Charleston before, remember? Ready to stick with me a few days?"

Mercedes gave him a sidelong look and smiled. "Looking forward to it! By the way, what changed about your schedule? I thought you had an online meeting and consultation with an archaeologist in St. Augustine?"

Quincy hesitated, then changed lanes on the interstate while buying time. "Stanley Lenoir is dead."

Beside him, Mercedes gasped. "But—he was in custody! How did this happen?"

"I'm waiting for more details. It was supposedly a suicide."

Mercedes shook her head vehemently. "Oh, no, it wasn't. Men like Lenoir don't commit suicide. They buy off lawyers and judges."

When he was quiet, she put her hand on his arm. "What aren't you telling me?"

She watched the muscles in his jaw flex before he answered her. "I can't say much. But my orders are to keep you close and to invite Jana and Declan down for a visit."

"How does Lenoir's death put me in danger? He's out of the picture."

"His son threatened revenge on you and Zach."

Mercedes stared at him, gaping. "You—you mean his son is after me now?"

"Maybe the threats were all bluster over his shock at his dad's arrest, but his death may trigger him to come after you."

She sat back in the passenger seat, digesting the possibilities. "Where does his son live?"

"My guess is he lives near the main office of the firm."

"Atlanta!" she exclaimed. "It's hard to believe that family followed mine all the way from England to harass us here in the States."

A light knock on the guest house door sent Quincy through the living room to answer. Zeke Ellison, Mercedes' older brother, greeted him on the porch and Quincy welcomed him inside.

"Sorry I couldn't make it home for dinner with the family," Zeke said. "I hear my sister may be in danger again. If not for you and her friends, we would have lost her that night in Hilton Head. I never had time to tell you in person how grateful I am, and I want you to know I appreciate you being with her now. You're in the line of fire for her again, so I put in for some time off from work for a few days to help. Will you resent it if I tag along with you two?"

Quincy blinked in surprise, then rushed to say Zeke was welcome to spend the days with them. "You may change your mind, though. We're planning to dig for treasure for a few days. It will be hot and dirty work."

Zeke laughed and leaned back into the comfortable sofa. "Just because it's been a few years since we were filthy with dust and stinking with sweat doesn't mean I've gotten too soft for it. I have a drone we can use and my equipment from the good old days when we had nothing better to do than explore the world."

"Those were fun times, but we had some evidence for where to dig back then. Now, we're looking for a needle in a haystack. Legends and conjecture are our only clues that there's anything to be found."

Sobering, Zeke met Quincy's eyes. "She'll be packing, and I don't mean a suitcase. You still carry?"

Quincy sighed and nodded. "Yeah, and it's part of the job now. I didn't tell her, but there's a possibility that they will encourage her and Zach to go into protective custody."

Zeke hissed and shook his head. "No. No way." He sat forward on the sofa. "She won't agree to it. Her business is getting off the ground, and unless I'm reading all the signs wrong, I think you'll be putting a ring on her hand soon."

Zach Boone rubbed the tension from his forehead and groaned when his cellphone rang. He was in no mood to talk.

Pushing his office chair back from his desk, he reached for a nearby bookcase where his phone sat in a charger easel. The scowl left his face when he saw who was calling. "Hey, Declan. I was gonna call you in a little while."

"So, you heard the news?"

Blowing out a deep sigh, Zach replied, "Yeah. Got the call a while ago and I'm sittin' here researching who Roland is. Looks like his dad wiggled him out of a few arrests and wasn't a candidate for Father of the Year."

"That's why we should take this seriously. Look, I've got an interview this week about an hour from Charleston and Jana's taking off from work to stay with Mercedes a few days. This may come to nothing, but why not leave town, too, just as a precaution? Travel with me, Zach, in case he comes looking for you. We'll stay awhile and get in some fishing and stuff."

"You're really narrowing your job choices to the Lowcountry area because of a woman you aren't even married to?"

Declan's tone was quiet. "I like it there. It's a great place to live."

Zach shrugged. "Yeah, I guess it is. Look, I don't want to run into Mercedes and her British aristocrat. Should I drive and meet you so you can go visit with Jana? Mercedes' parents live south of Charleston, near Kiawah. It's a long drive, even in that area."

"Yeah, we'll be scattered. I'll stay west of Charleston for the interview and Jana will work with Mercedes on a job at an old plantation north of Mount Pleasant, so it's not likely we'll meet up. At least I won't worry about her being alone up here in Virginia. You're back home in Myrtle Beach, right? If you'll give me your address or a place to meet, you can follow me down."

Distracted, Zach ran his fingers through his hair. "Yeah. Yeah, okay, let's do that. What's the name of the plantation where Mercedes is working?"

"Hmm, something about trees, those spreading ones with the crooked limbs and beardy stuff hanging on them."

"Live oaks?"

"Yeah! That's it. Majestic Oaks, or something grandiose like that. A bunch of them line a long driveway road to the mansion. She's helping the guy who inherited it do a historic evaluation and find the right agent. He wants to keep it but will have to sell to pay off his cousins, who were also in his uncle's will. Jana will help her and Quincy search around for some heirlooms buried on the property. By the way, he's an American citizen, born here because his mother is American and married the British aristocrat."

"Yeah, whatever," Zach growled, typing on his computer. A photo of Majestic Oaks Plantation popped up. He whistled. "I'm looking at it right now. Nice place. She'll love working on that project."

"So, let's get our own plan together. How much fishing gear have you got that will travel well?"

Roland Lenoir sat across from his pretty half-sister, munching a delicious dinner at her favorite restaurant. When he called her that morning, she was sympathetic and invited him to eat out to talk about his next steps after their dad's death. Her husband had not allowed him at their home in years.

He looked up from his plate to see her serene face watching him. She loved him, he knew, and cared about what happened to him. Despite having different mothers and being nothing alike, she was a wonderful sister who always made time for him when he needed to talk.

"You haven't been answering my text messages," she said. "Is there a special lady in your life taking up so much of your time?"

Her eyes teased him, and he swallowed a bite of his steak before he grinned. "No. I had a job, a temporary one. It ended yesterday."

Roland ducked his head back down and slid another bite of his dinner onto his fork. The job was no excuse for not responding to her when she reached out. Part of him wanted to talk, and a stronger part shunned her. It was like he had another personality that took over often in his life, but it never showed up when she was near him.

"Will you be okay until you find another one?" she asked.

He nodded. "Another job? Yeah, it shouldn't take long. I use the trust fund Dad gave me when I have to."

His sister sighed, and he knew her thoughts. She had not seen their dad in years and had no reason to. His father barely knew her, and the only reason she might be sad over his death was she believed his soul was "lost."

Roland put his fork down and stuffed back his sudden irritation. He looked up at her. "He didn't kill himself. I don't know whether there's laundered and illegal money in my trust fund, but there may not be anything left for us to inherit after the investigations, trials, and his current wife get through with whatever he left behind."

"You know how I feel about all that. You could never measure up to his expectations, Roland, and there's no need to keep acting out your frustration and grief about his rejection of all of us." She reached across the table with her hand outstretched. "Please, baby brother, let it go. Forgive him."

He blew out a breath and glanced around, leaving her hand empty on the tablecloth. "If I'd had more time, if he hadn't been arrested, I might've figured out how to get that land back. But he scorned me and chose that lawyer instead, from an illegitimate connection to the family. He was going to give him a partnership!"

His sister stretched her fingers out to him again in an appeal. "Let it go, Roland. He cursed everything he touched with an evil presence, and it's hanging around you, too. I sense it. I pray Stanley had a last-minute chance to reject that evil and accepted salvation from Jesus before departing this world. You can have that peace, as well. Let Jesus be your blood kin, the father you never had, the friend you need."

Rolling his eyes, he scoffed. "You never give up, do you?"

She smiled sadly. "Never."

Reluctantly, he reached for her hand. "Thank you for trying, and for caring. I love you, but I don't believe that stuff. I don't know how, but I will get revenge for the vendetta that consumed him and cheated me out of having a relationship with him."

He saw the alarm in her eyes. "No, Roland. You will destroy yourself over an evil man with evil intentions. He failed—like his father and grandfather, all the way back to the man you're named for. It was cruel that he gave you the cursed name, hoping if he failed like his ancestors, you'd be the one who stole that stupid land back. What do you care about a place you've never seen in England? The young lady he tried to steal it from by manipulating a marriage into her archenemy's family—she's a victim, Roland! Zach's your dad's victim, as well. At least he was the better man, with the integrity to refuse the offer and walk away. Do what the young lawyer did that night, Roland. Walk away, forgive, I beg you. If not for your future, do it for love of your sister."

After promising he would think about all she said, she paid the bill for dinner, and they parted with a hug in the parking lot. With another half-hearted promise to think about all she said and to text her soon, he closed her car door and walked away to find his.

He was a few parking spaces away when he froze. Beside his car stood a man, but there was something unusual about him.

He kept a piercing stare on Roland that seemed to cut to his soul, making him terrified and ashamed.

A couple laughed together and passed him to get into a pickup. Roland glanced at them to step out of the way. When he looked back at his car, the guy was not there. Spinning on his heel, he searched the parking lot, but someone else leaving on a motorcycle was the only person he saw.

He opened his door and sat behind the wheel, looking all around. There was someone here a few minutes ago. He saw him as plain as he saw the couple who passed. More than that, the way the guy looked at him was not something he would imagine. His sister never drank alcohol, and he drank none around her, so they both had water with dinner. This was not inebriation or imagination.

Yet, he knew if he told anyone about the encounter, he could not even describe what he saw. All he remembered was his presence.

A lean man dressed in black holstered his pistol and flipped his motorcycle helmet visor down. In a British accent, he said curtly, "It's no good. I'll meet you."

"What happened?" The voice from the speakers in his helmet was calm.

The man mounted his motorcycle and dared to look back at his target. He blinked and took a deep breath. The strange man who stared at him was still there, shielding Roland Lenoir and his car. Those eyes pierced to his soul.

He started easing the motorcycle out of the parking lot and spoke into the microphone in his helmet. "Couldn't get a clean shot. A man was there with him."

"Just as well. I don't think he has the goods in his car yet. We'll catch him later."

Chapter 3

Mercedes loved her grandfather's study. It served as the library of the house, lined with bookcases displaying unusual and inspiring heirlooms and items from mission trips around the world. Out of consideration for their long-time housekeeper, whose job included dusting the shelves, books, and collected items, her grandfather kept boxes of his favorite things behind the cabinet doors in the bookcase storage and rotated the displayed ones seasonally. This meant there were fewer items to dust, and the library was alive, an inviting place that changed with the seasons, studies, and experiences in her grandfather's life.

Tonight, he was expecting her, and she walked through the glass library doors into the inviting room. She knew that the person she was when she entered would be wiser after she emerged.

Her grandparents were comfortable in the sitting area, bathed in the glow from nearby lamps. In her grandmother's lap was a well-worn scrapbook. Her grandfather sat close beside her as they shared the memories carefully preserved on the pages of the open volume, and they welcomed her as she joined them.

She bent to plant a kiss on her grandmother's silvery bobbed hairstyle. The fragrance of citrus shampoo refreshed her senses, and she smiled as she got cozy in a wide chair with rolled upholstered arms to embrace her. "I brought the journal with me," she announced, holding up her Great-Great- Grand

Aunt's diary for them to see. "It looks like you're enjoying memories as well. I haven't seen that scrapbook before."

"It's old, and we stored it away in a vault to preserve it," her grandfather said. "After what happened to you in Hilton Head and the experience you had in Savannah, we decided it was time to take out some items and pass them along. Your dad and mom thought it was my place to do it, while they talk to Zekie."

Mercedes bit her lip to keep from grinning in such a serious moment. Her brother, Ezekiel Vance Ellison, had been named after an ancestor, her namesake's father. Everyone called him Zeke, but her grandparents called him Zekie from the day he was born.

"When you have some time, darling, you're welcome to look through this," her grandmother said. "There's no hurry. We'll leave it on the sofa table here for you and Zekie. But we need to explain some things that may take a while tonight."

Her grandfather rose and went to his desk, where Mercedes noticed a black leather case that sat on it. With something like reverence, he picked up the unpretentious shape and carried it over, then put it on the sofa table before him. "Our Zekie, he would pack this differently than my ancestors packed it. He's not a country doctor who also serves as a lawyer, planter, counselor, evangelist, and whatever else they called him as he lived his life. This case was carried in times when the best treatments were both natural and spiritual, days when a person's faith was often the best medicine after a doctor did all he could. But it used to be stocked with things like garlic, which is a natural antibiotic and purifier, salt, which is a purifier, and some healing antiseptic vials and oils."

"The clasp," Mercedes said. "It's mentioned in my journal. Tell me what it means."

He fingered the clasp tenderly and his voice was as if he wandered into memories. "It was a special gift to our family from a grateful friend. The design is a silver shield of faith with crossed swords on it. The engraving behind the swords represents dark and light, evil and holiness, as a reminder that our battle is not against flesh and blood. Every time someone in our family carried this bag, that person remembered to be ready to face an unseen enemy."

He pushed the silver clasp, and a click opened the case. Mercedes rose to look inside, then kneeled on the soft pile of the rug, her eyes scanning the pockets and slots where various antique physician's tools remained safely encased. A faint blend of both pleasant and acrid scents wafted from the tiny old bottles.

Her grandfather opened a pocket in the lining to take out a simple silver crucifix, scratched with use. Instinctively, she reached for it, and he laid it in her hand. "It's well worn, clutched in the hands of people we won't meet this side of heaven," he told her. "This helped whether people were faithful and found comfort from the reminder, or when they were superstitious and thought it was a charm that warded off the evil that was making them sick. It inspired them to trust Christ and in His work through the Christian doctor. These days, few people have any beliefs that would include the cross."

Then he pulled up a false bottom in the case. Mercedes gasped. He smiled indulgently. "Yes, your namesake aunt learned from the best about concealing things. There was always a good reason for it."

He drew out a silver dagger resting in a matching sheath. "The Ellisons used this as a tool, a sharp one. But they carried it for protection, as well. They traveled roads in dark places on dark nights and carried this in a pocket for quick use, not stored in the false bottom of the case. This one will belong to Zekie, with the bag. He'll probably have me return it to the vault."

After he replaced the dagger into the hidden compartment, Mercedes handed him the silver cross to tuck back into the lining pocket. Her grandfather took it, quickly tidied the contents of the case, and clasped it shut. Then he looked at her grandmother, who reached into a drawer in the sofa end table beside her. When she extended her arm to him, she held an elegant pearl-inlaid box.

The case was her brother's. Mercedes wondered if this box was for her, and sure enough, her grandfather held it before her as if presenting a gift. "The contents of this will need some explanation."

Breathless, she waited as he opened the hinged lid. The lining was faded blue silk, and against it lay a slender chain and silver cross pendant. The silver in the chain winked in the warm lamplight and the simple cross gleamed.

"Oh," she breathed, and held out her hand. Was this like the cross pendant that her namesake aunt had mentioned in her journal on the fateful night her beloved grandmother went to heaven?

"This necklace belonged to Claire Ellison. The one Mercedes had disappeared with her when she died in the bombing raid in World War II, and she was probably wearing it. Except for her necklace and wedding ring, everything else of value in the family was sent from England to America. The old cedar chest that showed up here in Charleston was shipped here at the time of her death and never arrived. We considered it lost. Whatever was packed inside was gone. But the deed and other papers in the hidden panel make it easy now for your dad to donate the land over there, and my gut tells me her lost journal is going to affect your life. So, the hope chest is priceless."

Mercedes sniffed and blinked back tears, recalling how she found the old cedar chest at a local estate auction with no idea something connected it to her family. It was not on the auction inventory list and a neighbor who stopped by told the auction company she saw a man unload it that morning before the sale began. Mercedes took it straight to her friend Sawyer's workshop, and while restoring it, he found the hidden panel and the contents behind it.

She looked up at her grandmother, who wore a serene smile. "Doesn't Claire's necklace belong to you?" she asked.

"No, child, it's been in the vault. I bravely married into the Ellison family, and oh, the stories I could tell! But I'm here to support and nurture your father and grandfather—and now, you, Mercedes. The calling that threads its way through the generations in this family is on you like a neon sign. We want you to be safe and to be prepared."

Her grandfather lifted the necklace and set the box on the table. She rose and pulled her long hair to the side as he came behind her to clasp it around her neck. "Claire Ellison was a rare jewel," he said. "She was more spiritually discerning and wise than the Ellisons when she married John, and her exploits with him were legendary in their time. They go unremembered in their country now. But she carried herself with such elegance and grace that only those who saw what happened believed the stories anyway, except for the ones who wrote books. She, John, and their son Ezekiel, your Great-Great Grand Aunt Mercedes' father, inspired authors who embraced the triumph of good over evil and allowed God to be supernatural, rather than molding Him into modern constraints of the visible world."

He came around to look her in the face, and her grandmother stood beside him. "Oh, my," she said, her eyes shining. "If the portraits in the vault are accurate, you look so much like her. I don't know how, after so many generations, but you do."

"She—she wore this necklace the night she was murdered," Mercedes said in a small voice. "She and her granddaughter talked about what it meant, that there was no supernatural power in silver or in a piece of metal."

Her grandfather nodded. "True. Here, sit down. I have something else for you."

Mercedes obediently went to sit beside her grandmother while he pulled out another false bottom in the pearl inlaid box. He laid the silk-covered piece down, then held up a dagger much like the one in Zeke's black case, but it was smaller.

She stared, open-mouthed and speechless. Was this *the* dagger, the one Stanley Lenoir had searched the world for? Was this the dagger that killed Roland Lenoir over a hundred and twenty years ago?

Her grandmother draped her arm around Mercedes' shoulders. "What do you notice first about how Deacon is holding it?"

Swallowing, Mercedes whispered, "It's a cross. The hilt and sheath form a cross."

With the kissing sound of a battle-honed blade leaving its sheath, her grandfather drew out the dagger for her to inspect. It gleamed and flashed in the lamplight as if the glow came from within the metal. Mercedes gulped and tentatively reached for it.

Sheathing the small weapon again, her grandfather solemnly put it in her hands. She studied the sheath and hilt as they shimmered and glittered in the low lights of the library. It was beautiful in silver, with a scattering of small pearls and tiny diamonds, perfect for a woman's hands. The dagger would fit into a normal pocket, like her cellphone did, but the hilt would rise out a bit from the top. And she now knew from family history that when used by someone who knew how, it was lethal.

With a small shudder, Mercedes looked up at her grandfather. She knew nothing of using such a weapon and wondered how she ever could.

He sighed. "After recent events, it was time to bring these out of the vault. We'll feel better if you carry this when you'll be away from home. Humor an old man. I can't shake the feeling that things may have come full circle. Lenoir named his son Roland, after the ancestor who murdered Claire. And he has sworn to lash out in revenge on you."

Quincy checked his cellphone again, waiting on a reply to his text. Zeke told him not to expect to see Mercedes tonight, for she would be with her grandparents. But he wanted to hear from her about progress on the plantation status and whether Jana and Declan could visit. He wanted to make plans for packing up for the treasure hunt tomorrow.

Who was he kidding? Sure, he wanted to check those things off his list. He was a list kind of guy. Do it, mark it off, go to the next thing. But what he really wanted was simply to have a connection with her. Tired as he was, he doubted he could sleep until he said goodnight to her.

"You've got it bad," he muttered to himself. Snatching up his car key fob, he marched to the front door of the guest house and stepped outside into an oncoming twilight. Under the guise of getting his metal water bottle from his cup holder to wash for tomorrow, he looked at the main house to see if the light was on in Mercedes' room. It was not.

Wresting the twist top from the thermos that sported a historical site logo, he swirled it to see if it was empty. He stared at her window from his driver's seat, willing the light to come on. But all he saw was the pink and orange vapor of sunset clouds reflected there.

An ache of longing clutched at his heart, wringing a sigh from deep within. Answering her brother about his intentions with Mercedes colored it all with so much intensity that he would need restraint to give her space. Zeke was like an American cowboy who appreciated action and saw no need to wait, but the British half of Quincy's upbringing dictated that a socially acceptable amount of time pass between Mercedes' breakup with him and his entrance back into her life.

He swallowed hard and tore his eyes from her window.

Mercedes settled into a comfortable chair and listened raptly to her grandfather talking about her Great-Great Grand Aunt, who died shortly before his birth. She was his grandfather's sister and his father's aunt, so he heard stories about her as he grew up.

"So, she was a remarkable woman," he said, summarizing his descriptions of her life. "Her father's heart was broken when her grandmother died that night, and while he remained at the house, he protected her from Roland's son by setting her up to live with her brother in London. It was there that she met her husband, a friend of her brother's and a physician, at the end of the Victorian era and beginning of the Edwardian. Society changed rapidly in the nine years of Edward's reign. They tried to adapt in opportunities at mission work. Her husband lost his life in the Great War, and she never remarried before she died in a Second World War air raid. My father told me sometimes she wrote in journals about the unusual things she encountered, but then she destroyed them before the second war. She told my father her experiences in missions and in nursing work would be misconstrued by a society that was fascinated with occult things, or religious leaders would label her as an eccentric who was too dangerous to work with faith organizations."

They sat silent for a few moments, then her grandmother asked about the journal. "She kept and hid the journal from the time of her grandmother's death," she said. "Does that mean she hoped family members would read it? Or do you think she assumed no other eyes would see it before she destroyed it, as she did the others?"

Her grandfather cleared his throat. "It's up to Mercedes. The old cedar chest came to her, and her instincts should direct her actions about it."

Mercedes looked from one to the other, then down at the journal. "My only hesitation in reading it is because I know it will change me. I resented it coming to me at first because I was trying to run from being an Ellison, to escape to living a more normal life. But I can't deny the miraculous circumstances under which it came to me, or how I found peace in acceptance of who I am after reading Mercedes' account of time spent with Claire barely an hour before she left this earth."

She sighed and opened it. "Let's hear what she has to say about her grandmother's death." After clearing her throat, Mercedes read the journal entry aloud.

I have been too grief-stricken to write anything. My incredible grandmother has passed from this life, and I need her more than ever. I will never be the same.

She tried to prepare me for such a time, but I was not ready to be parted. It was not unusual for my father to be called away, as he was that night. The local physician was dealing with a complicated delivery of a baby, trying to save the lives of both mother and child. A messenger came to beg my father to handle a strange emergency elsewhere, for someone who might have lost his life without my father's care. He spared that man's life but couldn't save his mother's. This is a bitter irony to him.

They have sent me to live in London with my brother. I don't like it here and can't imagine I ever will. But Papa says I'm in danger after the threats against me, and his heart will not bear another tragic loss or marriage to Lenoir's cruel son. My brother has changed for the better since losing my grandmother.

The modern medical and religious education he's had in London was creating distance between him and our family. But after reading the eyewitness accounts of what passed when our grandmother was killed, he has come back to his Christian faith and belief in the supernatural. He still wants to call London home and work here. Papa must run things on our land now.

Concerning those official eyewitness reports of the confrontation between my dear grandmother and the man who murdered her, I believe them. I know they are true. Yes, they are fantastic, but anyone who refuses to believe what people saw and heard with their own eyes knows nothing of my grandmother. Others in the countryside will certainly believe them, for the name of Claire Ellison is special. They would have expected her death to be nothing less than a story worth retelling.

Guards who have been loyal to our family for many years, a butler and staff who have been with us for decades, and even locals who were on horseback among Lenoir's gang that night all tell a similar tale. There is no dispute. The entire scene was a supernatural one, a confrontation between light and dark forces. The storm was unlike any weather phenomenon we have in the countryside. Men with Lenoir swear they almost didn't ride with him after they saw his eyes gleam like a demon before they left, and all who saw him challenge my grandmother said it was not those two, but a dark being and a light being who were in conflict.

It does not surprise me that a light being stood with my grandmother, as they swear. She has told me before that in a few dire situations in her life, she prayed for help, and someone joined her. It defied her ability to describe him afterwards, but he was familiar, and she felt safe with him. She believed it was a being in the heavenly host, like an angel, the kind in the Bible. Before the being left her, something unexplainable always occurred. It reminds me of how we may entertain angels unaware.

I looked up 2 Kings 6:16-17 tonight. While it's true that I may grasp at any comfort to help my broken heart and grief, it is undeniable that situations most people never see, are never aware of, are happening all around us. My dear grandmother was unafraid, as Elijah was in this passage, for she knew help was near. And despite my pain, I smile through tears at her courage. Anyone who knew her would expect that she would invite her enemy to know Jesus. She had been praying for Roland Lenoir before he arrived that night.

It was unexpected for me to hear that my grandmother stabbed her murderer before she died. Some will see this as a contradiction, for Christians are not to murder a fellow human being. She cannot explain herself now, but I have speculations about why she would do such a thing. In scripture, killing another human happened in situations of self-defense and justice. I also believe this has something to do with the beings with her and Lenoir. They gave him a last chance to repent; he refused, and the demon he allowed in his life lost his human host.

If my grandmother's silver dagger was not already a curiosity in the countryside, it will stir spectacular legends now. Superstitious people live in that area, people who believe silver purifies blood from the curses of monsters. Witnesses say that after she and Lenoir fell, and he drew his last breath, she reached over to pull her silver dagger from his heart. It was in her hand as she died. The police report says there was blood on Roland's clothing, but they found no wound on him. And her silver dagger was clean.

Officially, the cause of Roland Lenoir's death is a heart attack, and the coroner prefers to believe the blood came from my grandmother's gunshot wound. He claims the eerie flashing lightning and dark shadows of the night made everything difficult to see, and that my grandmother did not actually stab Lenoir. Perhaps she fell against him, and the blood on his torso was hers. I cannot say.

Witnesses from both sides of the conflict swear that a dark mist rose from Lenoir's body and fled the scene, chasing the horsemen. They believe it was looking for a new host, like the demons in Scripture, when Jesus sent them into pigs. Again, this is something I cannot speak to. But I don't find it hard to believe.

In London, citizens around me have lost any acceptance of invisible things, unless you talk about the occult, seances, and sensational occurrences they can manipulate to serve themselves or provide forbidden knowledge, which is witchcraft. They don't regard the verses in the Bible about spiritual warfare and that our battle is not with flesh and blood. But they embrace other truths in Scripture, comfortable things like love and compassion.

I am weary and heartsick. When I write here again, I hope Jesus will give me the mercy, grace, contentment, and joy that I know will come as I abide in Him.

Quincy's phone vibrated and the special notification sound for Mercedes chimed. Blinking the sleep from his eyes, he leaned forward on the sofa where he fell asleep listening to music in the romantic light of a small seashell-encrusted lamp. He eagerly opened the text message.

Can you come to the window?

Wiping the last traces of sleepiness from his face with both hands, he stood and made his way to the side of the room, bumping into the soft sofa arm. When he looked through the open wooden slats of the indoor shutter blinds, Mercedes was silhouetted in her window, backlit by low light that made the edges of her hair glow.

He pulled the knob on the shutters and opened them, then waved lazily at her. She waved, then pointed at the back of the house.

His pulse rate shot up. He nodded, and she blew a kiss before turning from her window.

Quincy searched under a chair for his deck shoes and jerked them on. Then he pulled open a drawer in the sofa table and reached for a small flashlight before rushing out the back patio door.

"I'm scared," Mercedes said, looking out at the black river, where the moon hung over its distorted reflection. Lights from other piers and houses dotted the water's edge like a string of Christmas lights.

Quincy took her hand and leaned on the weatherworn pier railing, inhaling a deep breath of marshy air. "Is this about something you learned with your grandparents tonight?"

She nodded and reached into her pocket, then pulled something metallic from it. Moon and starlight played on carvings and jewels embedded in the hilt and sheath of a silver dagger.

He stared, open-mouthed. "They—they gave you *this*?" he finally stammered.

"Yes. And Claire Ellison's silver cross necklace. She wore it the night Lenoir killer her." She reached into her shirt collar to pull out the chain and pendant that draped from her neck. "My parents gave Zeke the mysterious old black case that gets mentioned in family stories. It has a larger cross, one that patients held for comfort, and get this—under a false bottom in the case is another silver dagger, larger and simpler than this one and still a size that fit in deep pockets back in those days for self-defense."

"Zeke has one of these, too?"

Mercedes nodded. "I suppose he'll ask them to put his back in the vault. He needs nothing in the old medical stuff, except to remember there was a time when his ancestors healed without modern technology. Quincy, we read the journal page from the perspective of my namesake as she poured out her broken heart over her grandmother's death. I've been thinking about this all wrong—logically, materially, not supernaturally. Have your parents ever shared with you what was in the police and coroner reports about that night? It's something you need to know about me, about my family."

He shook his head. "No. Tell me what happened."

She gave him a brief version of the events of that night and told him he was welcome to read the entry for himself. Then she held the sheathed dagger higher, staring at its glimmering design. "Quincy," she breathed, almost whispering. "Claire stabbed Lenoir in the heart with this, according to witnesses who admit the flashing lights of the electrical storm and all the distorted torchlight shadows may have fooled their eyes. Maybe she only held up the dagger, but regardless, he fell and died. She had the strength left to pull it from his heart and held it in her hand before she passed into heaven, according to witnesses, who believed she killed him. But the police and coroner found no sign of a wound on Lenoir's chest. They claim he died of a heart attack and the blood on his clothes must have been hers. Officially, Claire never killed Lenoir. He died of natural causes."

Mercedes looked up with apprehension in her eyes, meeting his. "What really happened? Did they see what they wanted to see? Who was the 'being' of light that witnesses claimed was beside her? And what does it mean that my grandparents asked me to carry it? They prayed a blessing over me and the dagger tonight. Quincy, I don't know how to use something like this, and don't want to! But my grandfather thinks the unusual arrival of the old cedar chest and its contents, and the incident with Stanley Lenoir at the beach, are clues that this drama in my family history is about to come full circle. He feels that an ultimate confrontation is at hand, and we have the blessing of a warning to expect it. I want to deny it, but I can't. I sense something is going to happen, too. And I know not to fear, but so much happened tonight that I'm shaken."

Quincy reached for her and pulled her close, unnerved. But she needed strength, not his confusion. "I can't pretend I know what to say right now," he murmured into her hair. "We need to pray about this and sleep on it. Don't ignore your instincts, though. Carry the dagger when you can. Wallace Hampton won't mind while we're at Majestic Oaks this week, though I can't imagine Lenoir's son will show up there."

She nodded into his shoulder. "Okay."

He ran a hand through the length of her hair down her back, then said, "Nothing you told me changes anything about our future from where I stand. I accepted the unusual as part of who you are a long time ago. You can't scare me off."

"But—I may die, like Claire did. The dagger didn't save her."

Quincy's heart jumped, but he covered the stab of fear by rubbing her back lightly. "It was her time. If the stories I've heard about her and her husband John are true, the dagger saved her life up until that day. It's my job to try to protect you until the threat is over. Zeke is planning to help me if he gets the time off."

Mercedes pulled back so she could lock eyes with him. "If the fight is not merely against flesh and blood, in the end, no weapon I can hold in my hand will help me. Only Jesus can."

Chapter 4

The next morning promised glorious weather. A cool front was coming through, unusual but welcome in the humid summers of Charleston. Zeke piled in some final items for the treasure hunt into his sister's jeep. "I'm driving," he announced.

Mercedes rolled her eyes and climbed into the back seat. "Okay, you two sit in the front so I can have some peace." Reaching for her tablet, she readied herself for getting some work done.

Quincy grinned and came around from checking everything they packed and closing the back. He turned to wink at her after he got into the passenger side. "She has a long day ahead with us, Zeke."

Zeke laughed as he set the navigation for the Majestic Oaks Plantation. Then he looked in the rearview mirror at his baby sister. "It's been a while since we spent a working day together. I challenge her to find treasure before I do."

"Okay, Zekie, be the first to find something Wallace can sell to buy out his cousins."

Her brother groaned loudly when she used his grandparents' nickname for him. "That won't go unpunished. Expect to pay."

"Yeah, yeah," she muttered, investigating her email on the tablet screen. Quincy searched for a satellite radio station Zeke told him to put on. Then she said, "Yikes!"

Quincy glanced back. "What's up?"

"Um—well, some private information about the real estate situation Wallace is deciding on. I'll be recommending another agent today. Something shady was going on behind the scenes with his cousin trying to influence the agent he wanted Wallace to sign with, to accept that low offer Wallace mentioned to us."

Her brother exaggerated a sniff of the air as he drove onto the main road. "Anybody else smell greed? This cousin needs money, and he wants it right now."

"Not only greed. I caught a strong whiff of selfishness," said Quincy. "This cousin cares nothing for the true value of the property or for the best interests for Wallace and the other cousin."

"Right," Mercedes said. "He has never met Wallace and the other cousin, nor has he ever seen the plantation. What is it about inheritance that sets family members at odds with one another? I've heard and seen the most heart-wrenching true stories."

"And I've seen it happen at the hospital, right in front of me, before the person is dead," Zeke said solemnly. "I can tell these relatives have nothing in common but the hope of a payoff someday. Afterwards, they don't speak to each other again unless they decide to show up at one another's funerals. Even a funeral is a rare event anymore."

Quincy snorted. "Having a family is rare anymore. Weddings are rare, adultery and divorce are common, and kids have so many blended home situations they don't know how to think of what a loving family life would be like. Little wonder everyone is so dysfunctional and disconnected."

Mercedes sighed, looking at the passing scenery from her window. "It makes me hurt for Wallace. I don't know him, but he has a wife and kids of his own and he's a Christian. He's out of his element with all this. Will you guys pray I'll have the wisdom to direct him to a best outcome for everyone involved? My job isn't to cause a family war, but they hired me to evaluate the property, and the cousins may interfere."

"Sure. Is all the paperwork in order with the attorneys for the estate?" asked her brother.

"No. They couldn't get to it until now and they have a window of time set aside to finish, which is why I got the job. This is over my reputation level. I need to be sharp about it if I want a recommendation to future clients."

Roland Lenoir needed to lie low. People were trying to keep tabs on him, but he decided he was clever enough to dodge them and carry out his plan. Nothing mattered past that night. He left his phone where he lived and carried the one his father stashed away. It was on the law firm account as a general phone, not in his father's name, and law enforcement who searched his father's home and office could not find things like this that Roland knew about.

Last night, he pulled his car into a hotel outside of Charleston, South Carolina—not one that people would expect his father's son to stay at, but not bad. During the check-in process, he had his laptop case across his shoulder and posed as a business manager traveling with his company. The young lady at the front desk flirted with him in a darling, drawling Southern accent. He noted to himself that she wore no wedding ring and asked her about places to eat dinner nearby. She seemed delighted to help and recommended a few restaurants based on what his tastes might be. There was fast food, local diner food, steakhouse food, and fine dining, all within five minutes of the hotel.

No one waited in line behind him. With his most charming grin, he asked her which one she would eat at if she could have dinner with him. She laughed and said she had to work until late that day, but named her favorite one. He said, "I'll chose the steakhouse tonight so you can join me tomorrow at your favorite."

Today, he sat at a workstation in the hotel, solidifying his persona as a traveling professional. Other staff would see him and not be suspicious if she asked about his coming and going that day. She did not commit to going out to dinner with him tonight, but her eyes accepted. The young lady would fit perfectly into his plan.

Using the hotel internet connection, he confirmed the information in his father's thumb drive file on Zach Boone and Mercedes Ellison. It would take a little creativity to get her where he wanted to at exactly the right time, but he had a plan for Zach.

Zeke, Quincy, and Mercedes pulled into the parking lot at the nurseries and employee parking lot at the Majestic Oaks Plantation. It was busier than they expected, but Wallace Hampton waved at them and finished up with instructions to some of the landscaping staff. Then he trotted over to meet Zeke and help unload the Jeep. He turned to Quincy. "I got your email through Mercedes this morning. I appreciate the contract and will sign it."

Quincy nodded. "You understand it's only for insurance purposes in case of accidents. We may find nothing, but if we provide a report of Colonial Archaeology to help you with a market appraisal for the plantation, or give you some extra assets, we're glad to help. I'll be honest, this isn't how I usually work. I start with a lot of evidence of a potential cache—uh, a collection of material culture, physical objects people leave behind. If you've remembered anything that might help, we could use pointers in a direction."

Wallace reached into his cargo shorts pocket for a paper, which he unfolded. "I brainstormed some notes last night and sketched out a map based on things I remember my family talking about. The dirt in the cellar floors puzzled me after you asked if the floor was originally dirt. That's not likely, and I think it's worth looking into to see if there's a paved floor under the dirt layer. We know things that could be carried off were raided by the British in the Revolution. But the other family heirlooms I wish I knew the whereabouts of were hidden for the family by slaves in the Civil War. I've tried thinking simply about these surroundings, as they would think, for they loved nature and stopped to look for meaning in much of it. But if they hid things based on their interpretation of instructions given them by the mistress of the house before she left for safety, or an overseer, the hiding place could have been more complicated, with a code for finding it. Those clues could be anywhere."

Zeke and Quincy studied the sketch. "I imagine the landscape has changed a lot. The waterline, as well," Quincy said.

"And we should consider where the invading troops looked," Zeke added. "If they thought of the slaves as thieves who would steal and hide things, they would already have searched the slave quarters and other obvious places. That's not likely our target area."

Wallace nodded. "Wherever you decide to start, if you get too hot, the cellars are cool. I'll be helping some out here, but when I can, I'll find you and see what I can do."

Mercedes got a crossbody bag out and tucked her tablet and phone into it. "Before I put on a hard hat and gloves, I need some photo records I didn't get yesterday. Wallace, can anyone let me into the house for pictures? I won't be long, then I'll join you all."

He raked his hand through his hair and pulled his ball cap back on. "The housekeeper is late today. How about we all go over and explore that hidden passageway until she arrives? You can get your photos and we'll start on the grounds after that."

Zeke kept turning his head for the views as Wallace led them up a path to the mansion. Quincy stepped close to Mercedes and took her hand as they followed, and she flashed him a smile that made his heart rate jump. For a moment, she was what he told her about at Alljoy Beach one sunset evening—the one who made time go into slow motion in his life. This setting, the step back into history, the wild beauty of the plantation, all seemed to show her off.

Mercedes went to get her needed photos while Wallace showed Zeke the house. Quincy wanted Zeke to see the Delft tiles on the fireplaces. Taking the wide, creaking treads of the Freedom Staircase, Mercedes went to the second floor and turned at the landing to remember the layout of the rooms.

She took a picture of the view down the stairs, then a closeup of the workmanship of the mahogany banister. One of the front bedrooms was next, and she passed old family portraits arranged over a settee and an antique table in the hallway to get to it. Pausing, she looked at the faces of people who once called Majestic Oaks home. An ache that defied description came over her and she felt a little breathless. Like most of the Lowcountry plantation mansions, this one had no record of an architect. Their owners planned them, built with affection and to taste, added to as family size and fortunes changed. If it rambled or one addition to the house seemed out of step with another, it was a stamp of personality. These residents lived, loved, learned, and endured within these walls and over this property.

She wished Wallace and his family could hang a family portrait here. With a full heart, she closed her eyes and prayed for Jesus' will about that wish.

Wandering into a bedroom she needed a photo of, she snapped a few views. When she turned to walk out again, her eye caught a faded, yellowed needlework picture in an antique wood frame on the wall. Going closer to examine it, she found a beautifully embroidered Bible verse with graceful scrollwork to encircle it. The scrollwork joined at the bottom, where a burning candle sat in a holder. She read the words aloud in a whisper. "*The Lord is my light and my salvation; whom shall I fear? The Lord is the strength of my life; of whom shall I be afraid?* Psalm 27:1."

Entwined in the lines of the candle holder handle were initials, and Mercedes wondered if the lady who created the piece with such skill had a reason to be afraid, or if she was a friend who gave the picture as a gift for someone who was. She bit her lip at the reminder. Last night, she told Quincy about her fear of having the silver dagger. This verse would be on her mind today as she became more comfortable carrying it. Whatever was passed on to her with the possession of the dagger, the promises of the Lord's presence in her life had not changed.

As she descended the Freedom Staircase, Mercedes stopped, overcome with—something. With one hand hovering like a butterfly on the balustrade, her other went instinctively to her pocket, where the silver dagger rested. Her eyes roamed the stairs, the hallway, the adjoining rooms, and the front doors. But she noticed nothing out of the way, nothing to discover, and nothing to make her wary.

Unwilling to leave the grip of her intuition, premonition, or an overactive imagination, she froze right where she stood and pulled out her logic. She stood on the seventh stair, and the board of the stair was like all the others. No special markings. There was nothing to note on the wall beside her, or along the wall the length of the stairs. The antique paintings in the stairway depicted the breathtaking beauty of the Lowcountry and the river, and one was of a patriotic Revolutionary War era scene.

Without moving from the stair, she looked over the balustrade, lightly dragging a fingertip over the polished mahogany. It looked exactly like the length of the railing going up the staircase. Things were old, but the housekeeper kept them spotless. There was not even a corner of peeling wallpaper to give anything away.

She drew a deep sigh and wondered why she touched the hilt of the dagger in her pocket. Unsettled, she quickly used that hand to tuck stray hair behind her ear and prayed. *What is it?*

The men's voices came from another room, and she knew they waited on her so the treasure hunt could begin. The feeling she had experienced lingered like a wafting fragrance, but she was past the initial impact of it. She remembered her moving experiences upstairs, when she prayed for Wallace's family portrait to be added to the gallery of former owners, and the insight she felt when reading the Bible verse. She was still feeling sentimental and coming down the legendary Freedom Staircase brought the feeling of history and destiny to a peek in her imagination.

Mercedes decided this was the best explanation for her brief interlude on the stairs, and she took slow steps down to the landing. Her phone notification for an incoming message went off, and she quickly pulled it from the shoulder case and checked. It was Jana.

I'm on my way down to visit, following Declan, and he will take a detour in Myrtle Beach to Zach's house. Zach is following him, and they will spend a couple of days together fishing after Declan's interview. I'll drive straight to meet you in a few hours. Will you be at work?

Mercedes typed her response. *Yes. Come to the address I gave you for the plantation and pull into the first driveway on a sandy road. It has a small wooden sign about landscaping and nurseries. If you miss it and arrive at a nice rock monument sign with the plantation name on it, you're in the driveway for the mansion, but park there anyway and let me know which place you ended up. I'm so happy you'll be here soon!*

Me, too! What are you working on today? What should I wear?

Mercedes selected a laughing face emoticon. *Whatever you have that looks like you're digging up treasure—or bodies. And remember, it's hot down here.*

Jana sent a hilarious photo of someone making a face that looked disgusted. *Is this how you treat all your guests?*

Only the best ones! I'm getting ready to explore a secret passage that no one has been inside in ages, and then go dig for silver and other heirlooms with Zeke, Quincy, and Wallace.

Okay then, if you survive, save me some treasure and I'll be there as soon as I can.

Mercedes found the rest of her team in the ballroom, where Zeke and Quincy marveled at the blue and white antique tiles around the seven-foot fireplace. Quincy came to stand beside Mercedes and returned her smile. "Jana's on her way," she told him. "Maybe the girls will solve all the puzzles."

Her brother groaned and laughed. "Yeah, I once heard a fun fact. Women are great archaeologists because of their natural ability to dig up the past."

Wallace laughed so hard he staggered back from the fireplace. "I won't comment on that fun fact, and I'm not picky about whether the guys or girls turn up with the treasure at Majestic Oaks. Let's explore the secret passage."

The housekeeper arrived and walked into the hallway just as the group was getting ready to open the secret passage. Clucking her tongue as if they were children embarking on a foolish mission, she told them to wait while she went for an old broom and dustmop to knock down cobwebs and anything spooky that they might encounter.

They examined a sketched house plan while waiting to be armed with the housekeeper's tools. Wallace pointed to where the opening of the passage was. "See here, that's where the patriots could escape if surprised by the British when they dropped by for the leavings of a plantation meal, or first aid, or a night protected from the ice and snow. The trap door leads to a ladder they could climb down into the cellar, then the ladder would be tucked away as if it hadn't been used."

"Did the family leave the passage as part of the history of the house, rather than opening it for more space?" asked Mercedes while Wallace reached into a drawer for flashlights in an antique buffet.

Nodding, Wallace handed out flashlights and accepted a broom from the housekeeper. "Yes. If the stories were true about who came through and needed this escape route from the redcoats, owners couldn't bring themselves to open it up, out of respect for the brave men and women who risked everything."

The housekeeper handed Zeke the dustmop and got her phone from her pocket, saying she was ready to make an emergency call when they fell through the rotted timbers. "Thanks for sticking close by and being concerned, Maisy," Wallace said with a wink at her.

She snorted delicately, and he turned to the invisible doorway. A small button camouflaged in the wallpaper's design would open it, and only someone who knew what to look for would know. He pushed twice to get it open and warned them to duck as they came through. "I left it open for several hours yesterday, to air it out, but we'll disturb the dust on the floors."

Wallace went first and Zeke followed him, prepared to be the ones who stumbled upon any problems. Mercedes followed and Quincy was last, while Maisey stood guard in the hallway.

They became engulfed in a close, shadowy atmosphere like a closet, with only the open door behind them and their flashlights in front to see by. Wood framing on the wall to the interior of the house was unfinished and open. The ceiling framing was high, like the rooms, and someone nailed bare pine planks down on the floor for a safer footing.

Mercedes coughed as Wallace knocked down cobwebs. She had no view of what was ahead, but her brother asked Wallace about the old, watery glass bottles on boards wedged in as narrow shelves in the framing.

"Oh, yes, I haven't thought about those in years. They're small because we once filled them with medicines, natural folk remedies, for anyone who needed them as they passed back out into the marshes. The men coming through the plantation tormented the redcoat troops with guerilla warfare tactics and sometimes got hurt. Look, there are some rusty old tweezers, scissors, and things people needed on the run. They knew they could come and go without telling the plantation owners, who were safer not knowing they were around. Every day, this inventory got checked and restocked if needed, with medicines, tools, dried food, and clothing like socks and boots, depending on the season. The Continental Army was cold and starving, it's true, but the patriots here at Majestic Oaks tried to keep the messengers healthy."

Mercedes caught her breath as her flashlight settled on a Bible verse. "Were scripture verses written to encourage the patriots?" she asked, her heart pounding.

"No, I hear they added those during the American Civil War," Wallace replied from up ahead of her. "I'm not sure how many of the men who came through here knew how to read and write. There's no record I know of about who wrote the verses or why. You'll find three or four of them around the passage."

Quincy was close to Mercedes, and his breath tickled her neck. "Someone traced these words lightly with chalk and then made them permanent with paint or ink and a thin brush. The person was well educated, if not the homeowner."

"Exactly what I was thinking," breathed Mercedes, awed at the find. "And it's not a message I'd choose for encouraging a soldier."

She asked Wallace if she could photograph the verses to think about later, and he agreed. He and Zeke had moved up ahead, talking about the contents of the shelves and hooks they found.

"You're thinking these are important?" Quincy ventured, holding his flashlight beam to the verse as Mercedes clicked a photo button.

"Yes. They're messages for someone. Otherwise, why go to the trouble?"

She found and photographed four verses before they joined Wallace and Zeke at the end of the passage, where they stood over an open trapdoor to the cellar.

"This is the back of the house now, but it used to be the front. The river was the main road people came to visit on. If the enemy came by water, the patriots could flee through the other door to the pine lands for cover. But if the troops arrived by land, they would have to escape through this passage and run to their hidden boats or swim. It was nearly impossible to catch them in their territory here in the Lowcountry."

Chapter 5

Jana arrived at Majestic Oaks before lunch was over. She ate her own packed lunch in the shade with Mercedes, Zeke, and Quincy while Wallace checked into matters with the plantation landscaping business.

"In the early part of the last century, neighbors around the plantation brought in over five hundred flowering plants, like shrubbery, trees, and vines," Mercedes told Jana. "Added to the many species already growing here in the gardens, this makes the plantation a superb source for the landscaping nurseries. So, they have garden crops and the greenhouses to support the place. That part could be separated from the mansion and sold, but Wallace's family has kept this land since the beginning and he wants it intact if possible."

"What's keeping him from living here himself?" Jana asked between bites of her lunch.

Quincy said, "His uncle died recently and left the plantation to him, but portions of money will go to two cousins. After all the expenses in the settlement, he doesn't have the capital to pay his cousins, and they won't wait. They want or need the money now."

Jana rolled her eyes. "Let me guess. They've never been here and lived on their own incomes before this, but suddenly have emergencies."

Zeke nodded. "Exactly. Instead of having an income from the profits here, they want a payoff from the get-go by selling it."

"To be fair, they told Wallace they need the money for medical expenses," Mercedes said. "But one is pushing him to accept a low offer through a real estate agent who has no experience with historic properties. Obviously, that cousin's motive is to get his hands on fast cash, not getting a higher payoff in the appraised market value."

Jana swallowed her last bite and wadded up her paper sandwich wrapper into a lunch bag. "Hmm. This situation is going down on my prayer list as a hot item. Tell me about the secret passageway. Did you all find any treasure in it?"

Quincy grinned. "It depends on what treasure is. I got a good American history lesson. Zeke learned about some field medicine in the Revolutionary War, and Mercedes discovered some Bible verses she believes are messages."

Jana's head jerked around to Mercedes. "No kidding? What are you thinking?"

Mercedes reached for her phone and pulled up the photo gallery. "Look at this. It's written in the King James version of the Bible by someone who not only knew how to write, but how to write with a thin paintbrush on boards like shiplap."

"How much better is it to get wisdom than gold! And to get understanding rather to be chosen than silver! Proverbs 16:16." Jana read the verse out loud. "The message is about wisdom and money."

"Yes, and Jana, the family silver and other heirlooms got hidden away during the Civil War while the owner was off on the battlefields. His family fled at some point and directed the slaves and employees to hide things that would get stolen in enemy raids, like the British did here decades earlier. After the Civil War ended, many of the people living here weren't interested in emancipation. This was home, and they stayed as free people to live and work here. They found many of the hidden items, but not the silver, and not the two large mirrors that were a wedding gift from French royalty in the 1800s. There is also some inventory listed for antique Delft tile that Quincy would love to find. Some people who hid things may have passed away during that time, and others probably left. Perhaps they took the missing items, but the owners decided that the people who hid things forgot where those were."

"Are you suggesting these verses are about the location of buried treasure, like a riddle?" asked Zeke with a puzzled look. "Why write it in the hidden passage?"

"Because only certain people knew about the passage, where the hints were," said Jana matter-of-factly. "Unless the house burned down, it was the most enduring place to store valuable information. Pieces of paper would get thrown away with no one realizing the implications."

Mercedes pulled a sketched map from her pocket and unfolded it to show Jana. "This is roughly the plantation and structures that aren't overtaken by forest and marsh. Look here."

Beside her, Jana narrowed her eyes. "What's that? A cemetery?"

"Yes, for the slaves and freed people. They set land aside especially for them and it has a road for visitors. It also has the ruins of a church, or chapel, or whatever the locals here may have called it. In the verse I showed you, where would you seek the wisdom and understanding that's better than silver and gold?"

Wide-eyed, Jana gave her answer at the same time Quincy did. "In church!"

Mercedes nodded. "Right, unless a family member left hints in the margins of a Bible. But Wallace has no family Bible dating from that time."

Jana's eyes sparkled. "Show us the other verses and tell us your theories."

Picking her phone back up, Mercedes selected the next photo and handed it to her friend, who read it to everyone. "*A good name is rather to be chosen than great riches, and loving favor rather than silver and gold.* Proverbs 22:1."

"More references to silver and gold," said Zeke, raising his brows. "Could the numbers in the Scripture mean anything?"

"Maybe, but we'd do well to stick with simplicity." said Mercedes. "How about the word 'name'?"

Quincy slapped his thigh and leaned forward. "We should ask Wallace about the location of signs for the plantation back then. There's an old rock one with the name on it, directing visitors down the oak-lined driveway. Someone could bury things there and hide it with flowers, shrubbery, or other things they put on top of it."

"What's the next one?" Zeke asked Jana with an eager expression. Watching them, Mercedes smiled, and Jana selected the next photo. "*Examine yourselves, whether ye be in the faith; prove your own selves.* 2 Corinthians 13:5."

Zeke's mouth dropped open, and he locked eyes with Quincy. In unison, they exclaimed, "Corinthian columns!"

"Find two Corinthian columns somewhere on the property. That's where those two mirrors may be," said

Mercedes. "*Examine yourselves* sounds like a good reference to a mirror."

"But the columns on the portico are simple ones for the Georgian architecture," Quincy mused. "Wouldn't they keep to that style all over the plantation?"

"Maybe, but not in art hanging around the house, or in garden sculptures," said Mercedes. "Remember, we're guessing. We have no other leads, so why not try? There's always the drone as our backup to spy from the sky if we fail."

Jana cleared her throat. "Listen up, everyone. Here's your last clue. *But he answered and said, It is written, Man shall not live by bread alone, but by every word that proceedeth out of the mouth of God.* Matthew 4:4."

Quincy looked at Mercedes and exclaimed, "Many of the tiles around the fireplaces had Bible scenes on them!"

Leaning forward, Jana said, "Bread. That's a key word. Man can't live by bread alone. He needs the word of God. We need to brainstorm where the link to bread is."

Mercedes sighed. "Wallace may give us insight about that. But off the top of my head, what about where they served bread outdoors, to the workers? Or, where they made it, like the outdoor kitchen?"

Zeke rubbed his hands across his face and reached for his water bottle. Quincy blew out a deep breath and said, "Okay, this is a totally different direction than I meant to take today. I thought we'd be using equipment to scout out probable sites for burying things. But if everyone agrees about this, I'm willing to stop the archaeology approach and go with the clues and treasure map angle. It's a long shot, but after all—it could be fun, like those geocache trips, only without a GPS to help."

Jana laughed and bumped her shoulder against her friend. "GPS can't hold a candle to Scripture and imagination, right, Mercedes? Let's try it."

Standing up, Zeke grinned. "I'm skeptical, but my day became infinitely more interesting when my sister proposed this possibility. I want to divide up the clues between the guys and dolls to see who wins, but since I'm here to help protect the dolls from danger, I can't very well let them run around like they own the place. Besides, it wouldn't be fair to let all the women's intuition be on one team."

"Good! Let's do this for Wallace and the plantation," said Mercedes as she rose to her feet. "If we find anything that will help him pay off the pesky relatives, that's a greater good."

Quincy grabbed her hand and reached for Jana's. Zeke grasped both girls' hands to create a circle under the tangled moss hanging from the ancient oak. "In that light, let's pray about the outcome. Whether we find any of the buried goods from the house or not, we want Jesus to bless this plantation and provide Wallace with a miracle to keep it."

Zach and Declan checked into their hotel and wolfed down homemade chicken salad sandwiches from a cooler. They were in a hurry to get in a few hours of fishing at a place Declan heard about. The drive was relaxing until they reached Mt. Pleasant and Charleston, then Zach's stress level soared. He knew fishing would calm his spirit.

As always, Declan was a champ at deflecting Zach's grumpiness. By the time they had eaten and put other food they packed into a fridge in their room, Zach's tension eased.

He was ready to enjoy time with his friend and away from dark turn his life had taken.

They got off the elevator on the ground floor and emerged in a discussion about which fish would be the most likely catch for the bait they brought. Several people waited to take their place in the elevator and there was some maneuvering in the hallway so everyone could get where they were going. Zach glanced toward the lobby area in passing and noticed a young man working with his laptop at a desk provided for guests.

The man turned away instantly and put his head down, focused on his keyboard. Zach hesitated, uneasy. Declan urged him to the front desk doors and Zach muttered he was coming.

"What is wrong with you?" Declan's voice revealed his frustration as he and Zach loaded the fishing gear into Declan's trunk. "You're being spooky like Jana and Mercedes, only it doesn't mix well with your new brooding personality."

"Yeah, well, I just had a creepy experience in the lobby. There's something about a guy in there that isn't right."

Declan got in the driver's seat and looked at Zach with raised brows. "Not right, huh? Are you kidding me? That's going to be how we see ninety-five percent of the people we're around on any day."

"He reminds me of Lenoir, okay?" Zach blurted. "And he turned away when he saw me from the corner of his eye."

The expression on Declan's face changed, and Zach knew he hit a nerve. "Are you sure?"

Smirking, Zach said, "Dead sure. But it doesn't mean he's Lenoir's son. It means he looks like him. What are the chances we stay at the same hotel after he threatens to kill me, and maybe you? Don't let Jana know. I don't want Mercedes to be scared."

Declan controlled a shudder and swiped his hand over his face. "You haven't been the same since the night you talked to Stanley Lenoir in Hilton Head, Zach. All this really messed you up. And the trouble is, I have no assurances you aren't in danger, because authorities tell us you are—we are. I brought you here to escape the guy and may have led you right to him."

"We can handle this. It's a long shot that it's him. Let's go back and get coffee or water in the lobby."

They got out of Declan's car and went back inside, heading to the refreshments bar. But the lobby was empty.

"I saw a guy here, too," Declan murmured as they picked up water bottles. "You're right. There's something unsettling about this. If he's real, maybe we'll see him in passing when we get back."

"Yeah. Well, I know one thing that's real. I'm not going into some protection program over Lenoir's kid. He can't be that dangerous."

Egrets on the Ashley River at Charles Towne
By Pamela Poole
What the riverside at Majestic Oaks Plantation might look
like.

Chapter 6

Wallace came out to meet Mercedes' group and shook hands with Jana. Then he listened to the brief version of their brainstorming under the oak.

Pushing his ball cap back on his head, he drawled, "It's so simple, so unlikely, that it's brilliant. As far as I've ever heard of, no one in the family has considered the verses to be clues, like a treasure map."

He pointed out a shed where several golf carts sat and suggested they take them out to the cemetery and old church ruins. "Sounds like your first clue is the farthest away from the house. Let's get there while there's plenty of daylight."

After loading their gear into three large carts, the treasure hunters followed Wallace down sandy white roads that were often more like trails. Enchanted, Jana looked around at the pine forest, meadows, marshes, and cultivated fields. "It's like a land that defied time and lingered in the old days."

Some of the wild birds took the invasion of the golf carts as a curiosity, but they startled others into flight. Lizards darted from the tracks in the road and Mercedes pointed out some alligators sunning on the banks of a creek. Jana cringed, hoping out loud that none of them would guard the silver.

When they parked the carts by the old church, Wallace waved an arm over the rows of headstones and memorials, explaining that many had been wooden and no longer existed. Eventually, groundskeepers put rocks at the head of the unmarked, abandoned graves, with numbers carved or painted on them to correspond with records kept at a local parish. The cemetery always had caretakers to save it from being lost in the forest.

He led them through the crumbling brick foundations of an opening that was once a wide threshold to a small wooden church or chapel. Part of the foundations and a wall built of brick stood serenely under a blue summer sky.

"Why is the wall so thick?" asked Quincy, standing back to observe any tell-tale signs of the context he wanted for how the building was used. He noticed rust stains where four nails had once held something, and from the placement, he guessed it had been a large cross.

Wallace went to touch bricks on the foundation. "See how massive these are? That's what they built the plantations around here of. You can find them these days in people's gardens, taken from old illegal stills in the marshes. The owners of those stills stole—uh, repurposed—the bricks from the ruins of local plantations that once existed alongside Majestic Oaks. Anyway, I'm no brick mason and I'm guessing, but I think the builders based their wall thickness on the size of these blocks laying alongside each other. A wall will fall sooner if it has no thickness to it for balance."

Mercedes scrutinized the structure and traced a fingertip over the masonry. "The oversized clay-and-sand brick of the Lowcountry riverside brickyards weathers to a gorgeous, distinctive patina, but it has less structural strength than solid clay bricks. It's often necessary to build thick walls with them for multi-stories buildings, but I'm assuming this was only a ground level one. I think Wallace is onto something about working with the bulky mass of the bricks and adding enough width to the wall for durability."

Quincy tipped his head in her direction and grinned at the group. "I can't take her anywhere without proving how much smarter she is than me. And here I was wondering whether there was some superstition or symbolism associated with it."

Laughing before he shook his head, Wallace said, "If there was some symbolism about the wall, it's not noted in any documents left to me. People back then mixed their pet superstitions in with some basic Christianity and considered it truth, just like modern people do. The people who lived and worked here were close to nature and the rhythms of the tides, skies, and seasons. Time and numbers meant little to them, but they believed in bad omens and had a huge respect for the power of evil spirits."

Jana quipped, "Yeah, we've educated ourselves out of the recognition of the supernatural these days."

Quincy moved to stand beside Mercedes as she gazed over the church ruins and the old cemetery. "What are you thinking now?"

Her sudden smile was self-conscious, and she turned away to a view of the river in the distance. "Oh, nothing that helps with our quest. I was thinking about how there's something haunting about abandoned places. They were once loved, enjoyed, and considered permanent, until one day, they became lonely and in ruins."

Jana came to sit on some foundation bricks beside them, and her eyes found their view of the river. She murmured, "I feel that way, too, but I never tried to express it. I'm going to write it in my journal."

Wallace spoke with conviction. "That's precisely why I want to preserve Majestic Oaks. The Lowcountry doesn't need another resort, housing development, golf course, or shopping centers. We don't need another historic site park. This place needs a family to love and respect the legacy of patriotism, heroism, and endurance that has thrived here along with the wildlife and nature."

He waved an arm around the cemetery, and his voice caught. "I can't bear it, thinking of busy roads cutting across here and passengers making jokes about vengeful ghosts and thinking it would be a good place for a séance or Halloween party."

Wiping his face and sniffing, Wallace turned back to look at the ruins of the church wall. Zeke came near him, hands on hips, and said, "Let's do all we can about it and search for the silver."

Jana stood and slapped the sand from her jean shorts and hands. "Mercedes, what was the first verse you found written in the passage?"

Quincy and Mercedes stepped closer to the center of the old church. She took her phone from her pocket and found the photo. "Okay, here's the key message in Proverbs 16:16. It's better to get wisdom than gold, and to choose understanding instead of silver."

They discussed the merits of a few places in the foundations. But the brick wall remained the most enduring site for hiding anything, so they all took a section and inspected it.

"I think we should try using the numbers," suggested Zeke. "Something about bricks makes me want to count."

Quincy chuckled and said he was about to say the same thing. So, they started counting bricks from one edge, each of them on a front or back corner of the thick wall.

Jana pressed a fingertip to the sixteenth brick and explored above it. "Is everyone else seeing places where the mortar has crumbled away or cracked?"

"Yes, it's a characteristic of the wall," answered Zeke. "Look for a defined line all around a section."

"I have one!" she exclaimed. "Sixteen bricks up on the edge, sixteen bricks in. Proverbs 16:16."

The treasure hunters gathered around her. Wallace whistled. "Look, the mortar inside that area is a different color as well. Subtle, but something to note if you're really looking."

"Could this shot in the dark really hit the target? We need the tools from the golf cart," Mercedes said, running her fingers over the gaps between the sand and clay bricks.

"Don't get your hopes too high," warned her brother before he followed Quincy and Wallace.

"Yeah, Zeke's right, this is too easy," Mercedes mused. She explored the surrounding area, looking for more gaps, until the men returned with their safety gear and tools. "Guys, if the silver is inside the wall, it's stored in something. A framework would be necessary to support the weight of a box or other containers at that height."

Wallace studied the wall. "It's possible that the builders erected a framework like that, but they may have assumed the strength they needed was in the brick itself."

Jana suddenly thought of something and put her hand on Wallace's arm. "Oh! If we take out these bricks, can you restore the wall?"

He nodded and smiled. "No problem. I have friends who will do it."

The men chiseled at the bricks while the ladies stood back, sheltered under shade that stretched from a towering pine tree in the late afternoon sun. Mercedes had her camera ready for pictures and video work for the records on the property. She wanted to have a few for Quincy in hopes he would soon revive his archaeology blog.

When they got several of the bricks loosened and pulled out, Quincy explored inside the cavity they created. It was empty.

They loosened more brick around another edge. They found nothing.

Discouraged and hot, they stopped and went to the golf carts to get water from a cooler and rest in the shade. They threw their hats on the ground and Wallace splashed some of the refreshing water on his face. They said nothing because there was nothing to say.

Mercedes' heart fell as she watched the men walk away. With a tap on Jana's arm, she kept her voice low and said, "I don't know about you, but I'm not ready to give up. They're tired and hot. Did you notice there was no framework left where they looked? I want to chisel lower in case the wood failed, and the silver fell. If there's nothing there, let's examine the other sides of the wall again."

Jana's eyes were eager as they picked up hardhats, goggles, gloves, and tools. Selecting a spot with cracked mortar about a foot above the ground, they chiseled around the sixteenth bricks from the edge.

The tapping sounds of metal tools on stone reached the trio of weary men at the golf carts. Zeke rolled his eyes. "She's relentless and resourceful."

Quincy grinned. "Admit it, you appreciate those traits more than you hate them."

Zeke exaggerated a sigh. Wallace drained the last of the water in his bottle, and they followed his example. Then the men reluctantly left the shady shelter and took lazy steps into the sunshine. By the time they reached the old church wall, the tapping had stopped.

Mercedes glanced around at their arrival, then back to the loosened brickwork before her. Jana had removed a block and was wiggling one above it, trying not to break it as it came out.

Behind them, Quincy got his cellphone from a cargo pocket and squatted down to get a photo of their work straight on. Then he started a video. "You chose another spot on the wall to open up. What's on your mind?"

Mercedes glanced back, then realized he was recording. She turned slightly from her seat on the grass and looked at the camera. Pointing up at the area the men had worked in, she explained, "Our first opening was the best fit for the information we had. But a framework of some sort was necessary to hold the weight of the cache we're searching for, and there was none. If someone indeed hid a cache there at one time, they removed it, or the framework has given way after one hundred sixty years. Judging by the size of the container I'm expecting our find to be in, Jana and I started working from the bottom, where it may have fallen."

Jana suddenly yelped and drew back her gloved hand. Eyes wide, standing to shake off her shock, she told Mercedes there was an alligator in the wall.

Zeke howled with laughter and Wallace joined him. Quincy stopped the video because he was shaking with laughter, too. Jana smiled sheepishly. "I told Mercedes on the way here that I hoped an alligator wasn't guarding the silver. But I didn't expect it to happen!"

Mercedes grinned and gave her a reassuring look before twisting around to look at the men. "Quincy, are you ready to film this?"

He drew a deep breath to evaporate his mirth and steady himself in a filming position again. Mercedes turned the other way and called to Wallace. "We need a gator wrestler over here! Wallace, can you help us?"

Startled, Wallace sobered and stepped hesitantly over to squat down and look at the hole. "Let's remove a few more bricks and see how big that gator is," Mercedes said. Jana handed him her tools, but the crumbling mortar made the blocks of clay and sand easy for him to push and pull until they popped out.

When the hole was large enough, he peeked inside. Jerking his head to see Jana, he laughed. "She's right, there's a gator in the wall!"

He reached into the cavity with a gloved hand and felt around. "It's just a tanned gator skin, and too hardened into a shape to get it out. Someone wrapped it around something else for a layer of protection. But—there's a box shaped object under it."

Zeke gasped and came close enough to watch without getting into Quincy's video. Quincy rose slowly, keeping the phone camera steady, and crept forward to zoom in the view of Wallace getting more bricks out of his way. The hollow was growing in both size and promise.

Wallace tugged and brought out a leather case, cracked with age. They all stared at it before Mercedes nudged his arm. "Open it."

He set the case on the ground and Quincy came closer with the camera. Wallace tried the blackened old latches several times before they would let go and he lifted the top with protesting hinges. A carved wooden box was inside, its once-fine finish now wearing the years of storage in less-than-ideal conditions. He gingerly lifted the lid and found a velvety fabric layer, which he pulled back.

Quincy's viewfinder displayed the tarnished silver fitted snuggly in a tray, the elegant service from days when social grace and hospitality were the stuff of everyday life. Jana came closer and asked Wallace if she could pull the tray out to see what was under it. Dumbfounded, he nodded, and she revealed another layer of the lost heirloom silver.

"I don't know what to say," he murmured. "No one has seen this since about 1861."

"There's more in the wall," Mercedes said in a gentle tone. "Would you like to take it out?"

By the time they cleaned out the hollow in the wall, the silver tea service and several serving trays lay carefully placed on the grounds of the old church ruins. Zeke grabbed his sister into a bear hug. "I told you not to get your hopes too high, so you set them on the ground. Great call, Mercedes."

She smiled and hugged him. For his ears only, she said, "But Zekie, is it enough?"

Chapter 7

"Wallace needs a night of rest," Jana told the other treasure hunters. "He had a challenging day with a big job at the landscaping business and then an emotional afternoon. I'm glad we left him with the silver in the mansion and the housekeeper made him dinner. But he will not want to sell the silver to keep the house. Did you see the look on his face when he brought it in? It belongs there."

Quincy sat across from her at a restaurant table and put down his frosty glass of tea with lemon. "You're right. He still needs a miracle. When is his family coming up?"

"His wife and boys will visit this weekend," Mercedes said. "She's helping run his business in Georgia until they find out if he can sell it and move up here. The real estate agent I recommended called him, and they might talk tomorrow. What we find as we look for family heirlooms may delay him from signing any contracts. He's waiting on more paperwork from his uncle's attorneys, anyway. The guy has a lot to cope with right now."

Zeke's cellphone vibrated, and he checked to see who it was. Looking up, he said, "It's mom. She's a priority and then I promise to put this thing away. Looks like all she wants is assurance that Mercedes and I are together."

"I sent her a text to let her know we planned to have dinner in Mt. Pleasant, not too far from the plantation," Mercedes said. "I didn't know exactly where we'd decide to eat at the time we left."

Zeke sent a text and announced he filed a chaperone report and latitude and longitude with his parents. With a grin, he slid the phone back into his pocket, and the server loaded their table with food.

After closing the car door for his date, Roland Lenoir slid behind the wheel on the driver's side. The pretty front desk clerk smiled at him, content with a meal and dessert at her favorite local restaurant and happy to be with the guy he pretended to be. He smiled back as he started the engine and asked if she wanted to show him more of the local sights. If things were different, if he were that guy she imagined, she would be the girl he would look for. And his dad would hate her.

She was just describing a good boardwalk for viewing a marsh sunset when he looked up and snapped his fingers. "I can't believe it!"

Following his eyes, she saw two handsome young men standing outside the restaurant door, waiting for a text to tell them their table was ready. "You know them? We can go up and talk if you like."

Roland shook his head, but his eyes gleamed. "One of them is an old buddy from college, a prankster who got me good a few times." He reached for his cellphone. "Will you help me get him back? He's looking for a job with a law firm, and it would be fun if we set him up on a fake interview. This is my work phone, so he wouldn't recognize the number, but he'd know my voice. Will you pretend to be an agent arranging an interview for a firm using your service? I'll jot down the address to send him to."

His date laughed. "Okay, but if he's on to me, I'm confessing to helping his friend."

Roland knew the main parts of Zach Boone's resume by heart. He rushed to jot it down on a notepad in the console of his car and then found Zach's number in the contacts on his phone. He handed it to his date. "Use your professional voice, the way you checked me in at the hotel yesterday," he said. He pointed to a name on the pad and said, "Tell him you're with this agency. Then say that this other name, a firm in Charleston, wants to arrange an interview with him tomorrow. They can only make appointments after hours right now and can see him at six."

She touched the call icon, and the phone started ringing on Zach's end. They watched him reach into his pocket and study the number before answering. "Hello, Zach Boone speaking."

Roland could hardly believe the way his plan was working out. He watched the pretty desk clerk present Zach the request for an interview with a law firm that she helped with potential candidates. She confirmed his identity with assurance of hers, giving him the basic details and asking if he could arrive at six o'clock. He asked for her to send him a follow-up text with the address.

Triumphantly, she looked over at Roland. "You got him bad. But don't be mean. Tell him tomorrow before he wastes time showing up there."

Roland leaned over and kissed her. "You're my good luck charm. Anything you want to do tonight, let's do it. You deserve it!"

She beamed. "That's sweet! No one has ever called me that before."

He pulled away from her to put the car in reverse and leave the parking lot. Zach and his friend had gotten notification of their table being ready and started walking inside. Then Roland flinched. Out of nowhere, a man appeared behind them. He turned to look directly at Roland.

It was the man in the parking lot the night he had dinner with his sister. Yet, he was no man. His expression still challenged Roland to turn away from his intended path.

Roland tore his eyes away and backed out of his parking space. When he checked his rear-view mirror, the man was still there and still staring at him. He drew a shaky breath and drove between the parked cars, making his way to the road. His half-sister's voice filled his mind. *Walk away, Roland, forgive, I beg you.*

"Go straight across the intersection at the light," his date said from the passenger seat. He threw her a distracted smile and stopped when the signal turned red before they reached it. His sister must be praying. It was her fault the stranger kept showing up, and it irritated him.

He glanced in the rear-view mirror again, but this time, he had no view of the dreaded stranger. Another face was leering at him with unearthly eyes and a malignant grin. The one who never showed up when his sister was around.

Roland jerked his head to study the shadows in the back seat. It was empty. Beside him, his date raised her brows and asked if he was okay.

He nodded and managed his most charming smile. "Sure! Let's go see that romantic sunset."

"What are the odds we'd have interviews here the same day?" Declan said as they were led to their table for dinner. "Good thing you brought clothes for interviewing if you got calls from your other applications."

"Good thing I packed more than clothes," Zack muttered, and Declan looked at him sideways with a smirk.

"Yeah, nothing like a little assurance in the holster, right?" Declan said. They thanked the hostess and focused on their menus.

After a discussion about what to select for their meal, Zach looked around. "Too many things that defy the odds are happening. That call didn't feel right, but it's nothing I can describe. I'll look up the firm online. Maybe I'm just spooked after the incident at the hotel today. Or maybe I need counselling after all. I don't know anymore."

The cheerful server came to take their orders and pour fresh water into their glasses. "My interview is in the morning. After some fishing, I'll be glad to go with you to yours. Maybe the firm is interested in two candidates."

"You're a glutton for punishment. I already caught more fish than you did today. You want to try again tomorrow?"

"You bet I do!" Declan replied, reaching into his pocket to get his cellphone. "I just didn't have the right bait today. I'm solving that problem after my interview in the morning." He checked to see a message from Jana and opened it. "Hey, guess what? More good news! Jana's group found the family silver at Majestic Oaks after one hundred sixty years! Mercedes discovered some Bible verses written on the walls of a hidden passage they were exploring, and she took photos. She suggested they use the verses as clues for things that were hidden and missing, and the first one paid off."

He texted Jana to say he would call after dinner. Zach half-smiled with a pang of pride in Mercedes' accomplishment, and of loneliness at missing her. No one could have done a worse job of ending their relationship, and he was ashamed of how heartless he could be. He winced at a fleeting thought that came to him sometimes. *Maybe that trait came through Lenoir's blood in my veins.*

Wishing he had another chance to prove to Mercedes he was no coward, he picked up his glass and swallowed some water. Declan said, "Should I be concerned about Zeke, Mercedes' big brother? Is he single?"

Zach turned a rueful grin to Declan and decided to torment him. "Yes, he's single. He's the kind of guy everybody enjoys being around, so Jana will like him. And he's got money."

Declan winced. "Another strike against me. You know, with a sister like Mercedes, I bet he wouldn't joke around and call Jana spooky when she's having a moment of intuition."

Zach pursed his lips and looked away. The dining room was packed with people from many walks of life, and he knew few of them had the kind of encounters Mercedes Ellison had. Few sensed things the way Jana did, either. He wanted to be like the normal people all around him.

"You're right. I suppose people who live around Mercedes and Jana get used to living with the unexplainable things that tend to pop up around them. But I never would."

The lights on the dash were eerie in the dark as Quincy drove Mercedes home in her Jeep. Zeke had offered to ride with Jana rather than let the girls ride alone to the Ellison residence. They were all too much exhausted to celebrate the extraordinary day they had at Majestic Oaks, and with a good meal in their bellies, Quincy guessed it would be an early night when they arrived at home.

In the passenger seat, Mercedes was drowsy and quiet. With barely ten minutes left until they pulled into her family's driveway, his phone vibrated with a text message.

Mercedes opened her eyes. "Do you want me to check that for you?"

"It can wait a few more minutes while you get your beauty sleep. You might want it tomorrow for the camera."

She smiled indulgently and lightly slapped his shoulder. "I'm not asleep. Yet. But I will be as soon as I get to my bed."

"You won't send me a distress signal from your window and shamelessly invite me to meet you in the dark, without a chaperone?"

He did a double take at the look in her eyes and his heart jumped to the roof of the Jeep. But then she just smiled. "I'm too tired to be scared tonight." Then she did a Scarlett O'Hara imitation. "I'll think about that tomorrow. After all, tomorrow is another day."

Since they watched *Gone With the Wind* on their first night in Charleston after arriving for the job at Majestic Oaks, he remembered the quote and laughed while he drove slowly through the security gate in her family's neighborhood. In his rear-view mirror, he checked to be sure Jana's car was coming through. Zeke would need to tell the guard who he was and get Jana a pass.

Jana's car stopped at the gate, and he drove on to the Ellison house. After pulling slowly into the driveway, he parked the Jeep and reached to take Mercedes' hand in his. "I had been watching your house last night, hoping to talk to you. I fell asleep waiting. That was one of the most exciting things you've done—signaling me from your window. Do it again anytime. Someday, we won't need texts and window signals. We'll be together."

Her eyes searched his in that way that made him weak, but Jana's headlights in his mirror flashed and he let go of her hand. He went around to open her door and make sure she was safely out, carrying the things she needed from the Jeep for the night. Zeke helped Jana with her luggage.

His phone vibrated again, and he sighed before using his free hand to pull it from his pocket and key in his password. Then he stopped in his tracks on the sidewalk.

Mercedes turned back to him, and Zeke looked at him, his hand on the doorknob to open it for Jana. The look on Quincy's face made him pause.

"Is everything okay?" Zeke asked. The four of them stood bathed in the surreal shadows cast by the porch lights.

Quincy looked up. "They killed the guards. Lenoir's guards—the ones who meant to drown Mercedes. The prisoners were on their way to a more secure facility because of Lenoir's death."

Jana gasped. "Does—does this mean Lenoir's death was no suicide? Did someone kill all of them?"

Mercedes stood still, wearing a stunned expression. "Who do you mean by 'they' killed the guards, Quincy? Do 'they' have a reason to come after us, too?"

Closing his messages and putting his phone away, Quincy walked briskly up the sidewalk to them, glancing around. "Come on, let's get in the house. I honestly don't know what this means."

"Can I tell Declan about this?" asked Jana. "He's going to call me tonight."

Quincy nodded. He had ended a call and sat with Jana, Mercedes, and the Ellisons in the Carolina room, where he explained what happened. "Yes, but he and Zach will get a call anyway, so they won't find out about this on the news. Law enforcement now considers Roland to be in grave danger. The people behind these murders might believe Roland knows or heard something that will incriminate them. I'm only getting the briefest information, you understand, and only because I helped bring Lenoir Bassett and Madigan down for illegal antiquities dealings and for rescuing Mercedes from being murdered by the bodyguards. If the officers I worked for suspect anyone of killing Lenoir and his guards, they will not be forthcoming about it to me."

"So, all we know is that the guards were on the same hit list as Lenoir," said Dawson Ellison, Mercedes' father. "The justice system moved Bassett and Madigan to another facility before Lenoir, so law enforcement knew there was some security threat to all three. Maybe I've seen too much, or I read and watch too many suspense stories, but there's a possibility that someone on the inside arranged for Lenoir to be the last partner moved. Bassett and Madigan may not have enough incriminating evidence to threaten whoever staged Lenoir's suicide."

"But I don't have any incriminating evidence on any of them, either, nor do my friends," said Mercedes, putting down her cup of tea and shaking her head. "Surely there's no reason we would be on a hit list of such high stakes criminals."

"She has a significant point," Zeke said. "All Mercedes was going to do in the trial is tell what happened to her. She never saw who kidnapped and drugged her, then left her for dead to wash up on the beach in Hilton Head. She knows nothing. It's the evidence in the fishing boat and the officers' capture of the two thugs red-handed at the dock, thanks to Quincy, Jana, and Declan, that condemned them. They got hit today due to what they knew as Lenoir's inside team, not for a connection with Mercedes. She was Lenoir's personal vendetta."

Quincy sighed. "My employer agrees with that much, but he feels Lenoir's son and Zach Boone, as a distant relative, could still be targets. Zach's name is on papers as a future partner. For all I know, I'm the top hit among us because of my testimony."

Jana sat on the edge of her chair, wringing her hands. With a small voice, she said, "Does this mean we have to stop working to help Wallace at the plantation? He's running out of time."

"We'll find out what develops by morning when I check in. He mentioned the possibility of sending security for us if they suspect a specific threat by then."

Mercedes' father stood up. "Zeke let's go with Quincy to the guest cottage to grab his things to stay here tonight. I don't want him alone over there."

Roland's sister tried once again to call. It was normal for him to ignore her texts and she had seen him only a couple of nights ago, but she was nervous now. His voice told callers to leave messages, and she said, "Roland, please call me back! I've learned someone shot Stanley's bodyguards today and the police think you are in danger. They're looking for you and thought I may know where you are, but I don't. I hope you've given up on your plan for vengeance. Call me back and contact police so they can protect you. I love you, and you know I'm praying."

She swiped at tears and called her best friend from church. "Will you help me call some of our prayer group? Roland may be in danger, or he may be off on a quest to put others in danger. Either way, if he dies, there will be no more chances to determine his eternity. I just want to have peace that I did all I could about it."

Police knocked on the door of the apartment Roland Lenoir shared with a roommate. The roommate opened it, blinked, and took a step back. After introductions, the police said something had happened that concerned Roland and they had been trying to contact his cellphone. His roommate told them Roland had left two days before, saying he had some business out of town. "It's strange that he didn't take his phone, though. Little wonder you can't reach him."

"Are you saying he left without his phone and hasn't called you to check on it? If he's out of town on business, wouldn't those contacts be calling that number? Have you seen him use a different phone?"

The man shook his head in exasperation. "You'd think, right? I haven't seen him with another phone. I don't know, man. He's a weird guy, but clean cut and a good roommate overall. Minds his own business. I've only roomed with him a few months while I finished a job here, and I'm moving out in a couple weeks to work in another state. We barely see one another and aren't friends, we just cooperate to pay the bills, passing each other on our own schedules."

"Has he mentioned anything about his father, or about getting revenge against some people connected with him?"

The roommate snorted. "I hear him rambling sometimes, to himself. It's creepy. I heard him on some calls with one of his half-sisters, about his father, then heard about a case in the news and put two and two together. But I never mentioned it to Roland. Once, when he was talking to himself, he swore he would get the revenge they denied his father. It wasn't my business and to be frank, I didn't want to know what he was talking about."

"Thanks for your help," said one officer, leaving his card. "Roland may be in danger, and the phone he left may be important. If we don't find him soon, someone will be back with a warrant."

"I leave at five in the morning for work, but I'll give you my number if you need to contact me."

Chapter 8

Quincy slept well, surprising since he spent the night on a sofa in the Ellison house. He was that tired, he supposed, and after rising and getting dressed before anyone else but Mercedes' grandparents, he sat down with his phone and laptop to determine if it was safe to keep his plans for the day.

Deacon Ellison came quietly into the room and asked if he could bring him any breakfast. Quincy looked up to give him a quick smile and thanked him for his kindness. "I could use some hot tea if you have any. I'll just wait to eat with Mercedes when she comes down."

When Deacon hesitated, as if he wanted to say more, Quincy smiled encouragingly. Mercedes' grandfather was a guy who said things worth listening to. "Sure, my wife will make some tea and I'll bring it in soon. About last night, I just want to ask you to make sure my granddaughter doesn't forget to keep the dagger with her. Especially today."

Quincy's heart skipped a beat. He nodded slowly, keeping his eyes locked on Deacon's. "Yes, sir, I will. She doesn't really know how to use it, but like you, I'll feel better knowing she has it."

Deacon sighed. With a half-smile, almost of sadness, he said, "She will know what to do with it when the time comes."

He turned to leave the room. Quincy quickly said, "Mr. Ellison, should we stay home today?"

Mercedes' grandfather turned back. Slowly, hesitantly, he shook his head. "Do you remember when our families taught you, Zekie, and Mercedes to stay off the 'X'?"

"Yes, sir, I think of that lesson often and try to live by it. I'm sure it has kept me out of dangerous situations. The trouble is, sometimes it's unclear that an 'X' is in my path."

"And sometimes, your destiny is to be on an 'X'. For such a time as this."

Quincy blinked and drew a deep breath. He exhaled as Deacon turned to get his tea. Then he picked up his laptop and keyed in a search in his online Bible in the Easy-to-Read version, found it and said the words aloud. "God began by making one man, and from him he made all the different people who live everywhere in the world. He decided exactly when and where they would live. Acts 17:26."

There was so much in this verse, and it was one of his favorites. It was probably because of his interest in history and archaeology. But what struck him today was his reaction to Deacon Ellison's statement. Sometimes, the situations we face are for us, for a time we were born to, and outcomes we are uniquely prepared to handle as we walk with Jesus.

The verse reminded him of another point. The land that left the Lenoir family's possession and came into the stewardship of the Ellison family was God's. He would decide what happened to it.

Declan felt good about his interview. What he learned made him want to work for the small firm here and he hoped to be chosen from among other candidates.

He pulled off his suit coat and hung it in the back seat. As he got into his car and set the navigation to a local fishing bait shop, the weight of concern settled back over him. He felt the need to rush because Zach was alone in their hotel room. After hearing about the deaths of Stanley Lenoir's two bodyguards last night, he intended to keep his friend close by.

Turning the air conditioning higher and pulling off his tie, he texted Jana before leaving the parking lot. *The interview couldn't have gone better. I'm excited and I'll tell you more tonight over the phone. Let me know when you get back to Mercedes' house. Are you working on the plantation today or lying low?*

Jana's response was quick. She was riding with the group to Majestic Oaks. Quincy said Roland Lenoir was the most likely next target if there was one. Zach and even Quincy were next in consideration, and Mercedes, Jana, and Declan were the outer fringes of possibility now, because of being outsiders. *Roland is missing, and law enforcement now thinks he's hiding from the people who may have killed his father, because he left his personal cellphone at his apartment. If he's hiding, they think he will delay coming for Zach and Mercedes.*

Declan hesitated. *What are the chances he's hiding in Charleston?*

They think he's at a secluded place with few chances of being recognized.

Biting his lip, recalling Zach's request not to tell Jana about the strange experience the previous day, he sent a response. *They're guessing and could underestimate the guy. I hope they know what they're doing. Please, baby, be careful. You're always in my prayers.*

You, too, and you're in mine. Hope you have fun fishing. Jana signed off with a heart emoticon.

Before unloading their treasure-hunting gear, Quincy, Mercedes, Zeke, and Jana went looking for Wallace. The landscaping manager told them he went to the house to talk on the phone with his attorneys, so they walked up the path to the back of the mansion.

Wallace sat on the porch, head in his hands, and concern stabbed at Mercedes' heart. He looked up when they came closer.

"Is anything wrong?" asked Mercedes.

He sighed and wiped his hands over his face. "Complications. The attorneys had background checks done and gave me the results today. My uncle stipulated that any heirs to Majestic Oaks must have no criminal records and must be bloodline. My record is clear, but the cousin who wanted me to sell quickly has a criminal record. He's not disabled, like he told me on the phone, and that snake owes a lot of money in gambling debts. The other cousin, Mary, she isn't my cousin after all. She was born from a different father and her mom married one of my kin later."

Mercedes and Jana plopped down on either side of him, while Quincy and Zeke made a seat on the steps. "Oh, Wallace," said Mercedes. "Is she the cousin who looked after your uncle until he passed away?"

Wallace rolled his eyes. "Yeah. I never knew all the details except he was giving her part of his monthly retirement check as room, board, and transportation to doctors. She would only take him in if he put her in his will, which didn't sit well with me, since she lived on his retirement check instead of working. She also filed for caregiver benefits. He refused to come live with me and my wife because we run a business, and he thought he'd be a burden. I begged him to come, and I'd have sold the business to come here. But he wanted the friends who took over for him to have privacy and run the place without worrying about him. When he went to live with Mary last year, I called every week to talk to him."

Jana studied his profile. "Was your uncle happy there?"

"He was only happy here on the plantation. But he sounded content and settled and never told me anything I've learned this morning. His attorney just informed me that his home health nurse filed several complaints that while he wasn't being abused, he showed signs of neglect. I asked to see the paperwork about his time up there with her and hope to get it soon. But he passed away from natural causes, not neglect. He'd had a battle with cancer before going up there, and it took a big toll on him. Now, I find out she lied about why she wanted me to sell this place. My uncle's attorney said she has no grandbaby, no special-needs grandchild waiting for surgery that insurance won't cover. But Mary is planning to move out West somewhere to live with an online boyfriend."

Wallace snorted in disgust, then sniffed. His eyes reddened with unshed tears. "Why didn't I go up to see him? He died before I could arrange a trip. If I had any hint that something wasn't right, I'd have been up there in hours. He showed me photos of her house and I checked it out on the internet. But she was taking advantage of his situation, all for money. He must have been lonely."

Zeke said, "You probably want to give her a piece of your mind, Wallace, but don't speak to her. Things get out of hand quickly and you may say things she'll try to sue you over. Handle this through your uncle's lawyer. She may try to call you after the attorney's office notifies her of failure to meet your uncle's stipulations to inherit any of the estate in his will. Don't answer her calls. Let everyone cool off and the attorneys settle the legalities before anyone speaks to one another."

Wallace nodded. "Yeah, that's what the attorney said. But, despite what Mary's done, I appreciate she watched after him on a basic level. He swore he'd never go to a nursing facility, and he never had to. He paid her and yes, she tried to swindle us for more. I'd still like to give her a token amount of money. Maybe it will pay her travel expenses to move out West."

Bird songs and splashing in the nearby bird bath filled a few moments of silence while they all sat, considering Wallace's situation. Quincy said, "I think your uncle was shrewd and knew exactly what he was doing when he agreed to put Mary in his will, but then added a stipulation she didn't know about. I believe he knew your other cousin had a weak moral character and criminal record, and to give him money would be to flush it down the toilet. By adding these conditions to his will, he gave them no reason to blame you for being the sole heir. They could be furious with him, but not you. Both are paying their own consequences. You're reaping the blessings you sowed in his life."

Tears ran down Wallace's face now. "I miss him," he said in a strangled voice. "I'll do all I can to keep this place and make what's left of it thrive, for his legacy and the history that happened here."

He wiped his face with the back of his hand and turned to Mercedes. "Will you call the real estate agent and tell him I won't be putting the plantation on the market yet? I want to try to keep it."

She smiled. "Of course. Does this mean I've lost my job?"

Everyone laughed, and he said, "No, you'll be paid from the estate by the attorneys, so the records are caught up with all the state historic organizations and with property appraisals. But if you'll help me dig around some more for treasure, I can afford to share some of it now."

"How about you invest it back into the mansion and give us a lifetime pass to come here and hang out sometimes?" asked Mercedes.

He grinned. "Of course. What's our next clue and Bible verse?"

Roland Lenoir sat with a meal and his laptop on the table at a café near the hotel. He had anxiously checked out and would not be back there, for he wanted no loose ends. It was unlikely he would live to see tomorrow.

The television news was on in his room as he filled his suitcase, and he saw a brief report about the death of his father's two bodyguards. Roland had his hands on things the killers wanted, things his father had no time to get rid of. He also had his hands on a personal letter from his father that his stepmother gave him. Maybe he never lived up to his father's expectations, but there was still time to fulfill his last wish.

He opened his email to read while he ate. His half-sister sent one with a subject line that said she loved him.

With a roll of his eyes and a smile, he opened it. She told him she tried to call, and the police were looking for him. They suspected a criminal organization their father was part of had assassinated the bodyguards, and police feared Roland's life may be in danger next. She begged him to call her and to let police know where he was.

Maybe he would call her when it was too late to stop him. She would probably let him go to voicemail, since this number was not his. When she checked it, there would be a nice recording to remember him by.

"*A good name is rather to be chosen than great riches, and loving favor rather than silver and gold.* Proverbs 22:1," Mercedes said, reading the words from the photo she took in the hidden passage. The group stood at the rock monument marker that had long announced to visitors that they had arrived at Majestic Oaks.

Wallace pointed out the landscaping around the weathered rock with the chiseled name of the plantation carved into it. "As far back as I've seen in photos of the driveway, this rock was here, and they planted seasonal flowers to make the view cheerful."

Jana smiled. "Well, we know it proclaims a 'good name' so it's a good place to dig for buried treasure."

The rock was as tall as Mercedes' hip as she leaned against it. "We should take a group photo before we tear up the flower bed. Whether or not we find anything, we'll replant the flowers as they were."

The men dug in different places around the monument, and it was Zeke who hit something metallic with his shovel. The others came closer while he carefully worked around in the hole.

When he pushed the soil aside to see what looked like the lid of a plain metal box, Zeke asked Wallace to do the honors of pulling the object out. Quincy held up his camera to video the possible important find. With an effort, Wallace freed the box and brought it up to the ground at the foot of the sign for Majestic Oaks.

But the box had a quaint antique padlock on it. Without a key or tools, there was no way to open it. Barely containing his excitement, Wallace told them there was a stash of old keys at the house, and they filled the holes and replanted the flowers.

"What's the next clue?" asked Zeke as they marched up the driveway. "I hope it doesn't involve digging. I'll need lunch before I can do that again."

Mercedes read the verse from the next photo. "*Examine yourselves, whether ye be in the faith; prove your own selves.* 2 Corinthians 13:5."

"This is my favorite," said Quincy. "Now we look for something ancient, two Corinthian columns somewhere on the property, most likely outside. We're hoping to find two large mirrors. But if they buried something like those, they won't be in good shape. It would have been better to store them under the house in the cellar or standing up. Like, inside one of those thick brick walls."

"We'd have to knock the entire wall down to get them out," Zeke pointed out. "It would make sense to hide them out of the elements inside the house, but then, if the Yankees burned down the place, they'd be destroyed."

Wallace took the metal strongbox and went inside to find a key that fit the old padlock. The others went to get their water bottles for a break before searching for two Corinthian columns.

Mercedes, Jana, Zeke, and Quincy stood in the shade at the back of the Jeep, drinking water and eating apples before going on the next hunt for the lost plantation inventories. Jana looked around to be sure none of the landscaping personnel and customers were in earshot. "I'm glad we're here to distract Wallace. If he dwells on the situation with his uncle and Mary, and even with the way his gambling cousin tried to swindle him, he could be in a bad temper today. Like Zeke and his attorney advised, he needs to stand back and stay quiet. He's grieving for his uncle and feels he deserved better than his life with Mary."

"Yes, and I hope he'll come to accept that the choice was his uncle's," Mercedes said. "The way things turned out, I think his uncle was shrewd, like Quincy said. This way, Mary benefited a year's income from his uncle, and he learned firsthand whether she was a deserving heir. Perhaps if she'd been an attentive caregiver, he would have made another provision for her from the estate."

Zeke stood and dusted the sand from his shorts. "Let's see if we can brighten his morning by finding anything else. Two Corinthian columns intrigue me."

As they gathered their apple cores and found a trash bin, Jana admitted she needed a refresher on Corinthian architectural style. "We're not looking for simple columns, like the eight that support the front portico of the plantation, right?"

"Right," Mercedes said. "A Greek Corinthian style has fluted, slender columns. But the capitals—the crowns at the top—are decorative, adorned with things like acanthus leaves and scrollwork. Acanthus leaves have a medicinal value, and they symbolize long life when used in architecture. They're often carved in a stylized way, and some curl back."

Quincy pointed toward the river. "Mercedes, when Wallace gave us a tour a couple days ago, I thought I saw glimpses of a formal garden and a structure through the trees in the back—what was once the front yard, riverside. Let's try to find it."

They gathered tools they used on the brick wall in the church ruins the day before, and Zeke carried a shovel. Then they took a path of paver stones through hedges and found what had once been beautiful gardens. Quincy pointed at a kind of wall with a pretty sculpture decoration in the middle. "There it is!"

The group wiped away sweat from their foreheads, no longer shaded under the oaks as they were when digging around the entrance sign. They stopped to catch their breath, surveying the ghostly traces of planned walkways, seating, and sculpture. Now, a riot of blooming vines and misshapen, overgrown shrubbery ruled what was once a reprieve.

Jana sounded deflated. "I don't see any columns."

Mercedes pushed away branches along a path that led toward the river while her brother teased Jana by reminding her to watch out for snakes. Then she looked back, wondering about the view guests had when arriving on boats, and she gasped before shouting for Quincy.

The group ran to her, half afraid she got hurt and half excited that she may have found what they were looking for. She pointed at the wall on the other side.

Jana's hands came up over her mouth in shock. Zeke exclaimed, "No way!" Quincy breathed, "Thank you, Lord!"

The riverside view of the decorated brick wall was sheltered by a trellis over wide stone benches. Corinthian columns supported the trellis on each end.

"I can hardly believe my eyes," Jana murmured. In a stronger voice, she said, "It seems—impossible!" She and Mercedes tried to fight their way through the overgrowth to the columns, and the men followed them.

They found the benches had once looked to a large fountain, which was now full of seasons of debris from nearby trees. A graceful maiden wearing a modest, draping Greek dress held a large water jar from which clear, sparking refreshment cascaded down into the pool. Sculpted waterlilies, vines, and moss made a carpet for the maiden's slender bare feet.

Enchanted, Mercedes brushed off the marble bench seat between the columns and imagined what the garden must have been like. Quincy came to sit by her and grinned. "Has this distracted you from the possibility of finding the French mirrors?"

"He has to restore this secret garden," she said firmly. "It will take a lot of work, but he simply must do this. Wedding planners would get in line to take advantage of it."

"What a lovely place this must have been!" Jana exclaimed, coming up to them. "Can you imagine a wedding here?"

Mercedes and Quincy laughed. "Mercedes just said something like that. I think Wallace has overlooked another way to make the plantation support itself."

Zeke called for them. They found him studying the sides of the thick garden wall structure. He tapped on the vertical cypress panel walls and announced that the wall was hollow, like the other one at the church, except the sides were both made of painted wood.

"I'll text Wallace," Mercedes told them. "Can we remove either of those side panels without damaging the wall?"

Wallace quickly responded to her message, saying he was looking for them and was on his way. Quincy and Zeke found one side of the wall fastened with hinges, making the panel appear to open as a door.

"I'm not buying this yet," Zeke said, shaking his head. "Someone would have opened this in the last 160 years."

Quincy nodded. "But look at those hinges, Zeke. They're in no shape to work. We'll need to remove them. And there's no handle to pull out with, either."

Wallace jogged up to them, out of breath. "You won't believe this! I found the key for the lock on the strongbox. It took some oil worked in to make it open, but then I called my lawyer. There were some gold and silver coins inside and various papers. A few of them were stock certificates, and the attorney was contacting an agency who specializes in researching the value of old stocks. Four of them were from companies started in the early 1800s and they are still around today! I'm sure it will cost me to find out, but it's worth looking into. Banking, cosmetics and health products, tractors, and expensive décor. A few of those were risky stocks at the time they buried the box."

"Every undertaking in life is a risk," Quincy quipped, grinning. "And now you're faced with another one. Look on the other side of this wall."

Wallace made his way through strangling vines and branches toward the old fountain. "Hey, she's still here!" he exclaimed. "When I was a little boy, I was going to marry her."

They laughed at him, then Zeke said, "Look at the wall!"

Wallace turned, and his brows shot up. "Oh, man! Are those Corinthian columns? I didn't know, and I haven't been out here in so many years I forgot they were here! My uncle kept it up while my aunt was alive, but that was years ago, and he had his hands full trying to run the other aspects of the plantation to make it pay for itself. He couldn't afford a gardener to keep up such a time-intensive spot. It's more like a park than a garden."

"Oh, Wallace, he missed an opportunity!" Mercedes said. "If you restore this into formal gardens, it could be a showplace for your landscaping business and a popular place for weddings. Profits would pay off the cost of a gardener coming in sometimes to keep it tamed. Look over here, see where there could be spaces to show off blooming plants in season and switch them out? You wouldn't need to plant them in the ground, just set the plastic containers in the concrete planters."

"Speaking of profits, can we get back to the treasure hunt?" asked Zeke, and they all laughed.

Quincy beckoned Wallace over. "We have vertical wooden sides on this wall, three boards wide. This one has some rusted, painted hinges that aren't likely to function. There's no handle to pull it open. I can nail or drill something into the wood to open it or remove those hinges. You decide what happens next."

Wallace ran a hand over the weathered panel. "This could function as a narrow storage area for garden tools. Let's take the whole panel off. I have a collection of old hardware in the cellar, handmade stuff by the workers who once lived here. We can replace those hinges."

The men started working on opening the wall while Mercedes and Jana started clearing some of the tangle of vines near it. In half an hour, the panel was ready to be pulled off. As usual, they asked Wallace to make the discovery, and he did.

Standing upright, side by side, he uncovered the hidden French mirrors. After so many years, they needed some repairs, which Mercedes told him her friend Sawyer could come out to do. And someday soon, they would once again hang in their former glory in the Majestic Oaks Ballroom.

Jana was so excited about the discoveries at the plantation that she texted Declan about them, and about how the overjoyed housekeeper insisted on making lunch for them. *She worked with my diet limitations, so Mercedes and I ate a sensational salad and a chilled fruit salad dessert to die for!*

Astonished at their success, Declan sent a message back. *Congratulations! What a monumental day for Wallace! The return of the lost heirlooms is quite an accomplishment. I thought it would take days of digging if the items were still there. As for lunch, I had a less than healthy sandwich with Zach on our way to fish. We're wrapping up shortly. He has an unexpected interview in Charleston at six.*

Wow, really? Okay, I'll pray about it. Yeah, I think it says a lot about the character of the people who hid the valuables here that they didn't break the trust of the owner. Now, we are looking for some tiles. And we have one more Bible verse for that clue. Got to run now. We're back to business.

Fantastic! I'm proud of you, Jana, and I love you.

Jana sent him a heart emoticon. He smiled and turned to Zach as he put his phone away and picked up his fishing rod again. "She loves me."

He couldn't see Zach's eyes behind his sunglasses, but he wore a wry smile. "I'm happy for you, Declan," he said. I really am. And I hope this job you want will come through so you two can get married and live here."

Declan watched his fishing line in the blackwater swamp and thanked Zach. "By the way, they found the last two missing heirlooms that were hidden and forgotten," he said. "Mercedes was right. Those Bible verses in the hidden passage were clues. Crazy that no one ever thought of that all these years. The person who wrote them must have moved on or passed away before it was safe to bring the goods back into the house. That job Mercedes did in Savannah proved it was dangerous to have anything valuable around during and after the war."

Zach's expression behind his sunglasses was deadpan now. "If anyone thinks of or sees something as no one else would, it's Mercedes Ellison."

His line pulled taunt, and he started reeling in another fish. Declan said, "Exactly! Think of it, any other architectural historian on that job would have done as little as possible and gone, and the heirlooms would still be hidden. Now, they're looking at the last verse, hoping to find something Quincy is interested in, some old tiles with pictures painted on them." He had a fish on his line while Zach got his in and grunted with the effort. "They're going to work late, probably until dark. Want me to ride with you to your interview, then we'll go get something to eat? What about that place where all those famous people have a nameplate at the tables, marking where they once sat?"

Zack squatted by the water and slid his fish into it. The fish left in a flash of shimmering scales, and he remained there, watching the ripples. "Let's do that tomorrow night. We'll drive separately and you can go meet Jana somewhere."

Declan's fish almost flew out of his hands to land back in the water. He washed them off and grabbed his towel. "You still think there will be no interview."

Zach stood and wiped his hands, then pointed at his fishing bait. "I think the interview is the bait and I'm the fish. Pray I'm wrong."

"All the more reason for me to be with you."

"All the more reason for you *not* to be with me."

Declan threw down his fishing rod. "I've had it with you, Zach!"

Pulling his phone from his pocket, he looked up the name of the law firm and called them. Zach was uncertain what Declan was doing until he was asking the law firm to confirm his interview time at six that evening.

When there was no appointment on the schedule, he apologized and said he must have misunderstood the message from the agent working for him. He hit the icon for Jana's cellphone and while it rang, he said, "Now. That's over. Simple."

"How is that simple, Declan? I was going to do that much! Now, when I don't show up, this never-ending story drags on."

"Hi, beautiful," Declan said into his phone. "Listen, I know you said you guys are working late, and I wanted you to be extra careful tonight. We found out someone led Zach on a wild goose chase about having an interview, and I think the timing is creepy."

He looked over at Zach, who was also busy with his cellphone. When he got a pre-recorded generic voice asking him to leave a message, Declan heard him say, "The game's over. If you want to meet, don't hide behind a woman and false pretenses." Then Zach ended the call and shoved his phone into his pocket.

Jana asked if they were in a public place. When she found they were still fishing, with few people around, she suggested they go back to their hotel. "I'm telling Quincy about this. He'll report it."

He followed Zach's lead and started packing up his fishing gear. "We'll hang out in the room, watch a movie, and play an online game with our laptops," he said.

Zach sighed. "Sounds like we'll be calling for a pizza delivery. But remember, Roland may know where we're staying."

"Once we get to our room, he can't get in unless we let him," said Declan firmly. "Hopefully, by tomorrow, this will all be over."

Chapter 9

It was late afternoon when Jana got Declan's call and told her friends. While Quincy stepped out of earshot for a private conversation with his law enforcement connection about that information, Wallace came from checking in with the greenhouse crew and joined them. They listened as he pointed out the barn and livestock area of the property, showing them the cattle and chickens being raised for food. Scattered horses dotted a pastoral scene in a distant fenced pasture. "We're careful about secure fences for the livestock, especially at night," he told them. "There are some notes in the records about how large alligators have carried off a few young cattle and dogs around here in the past. My uncle never got another dog after the last one died of old age a couple of years ago, so that will be a priority of mine soon. Not much can top a big dog outside as a security alarm. Wish I had one now. It's dark and lonely here at night."

Quincy rejoined them and said nothing about his call, listening to Wallace tell them how the livestock on the plantation were far less than it had once been, since it only supported the family and people who paid to have their animals raised there as food. "Four of the horses are ours, but we board a few other horses off and on."

Soon, they turned back to the house, planning to explore the cellars and the next clue written in the passage. Walking around the plantation was an interaction with nature, and Wallace took a deep breath of fresh air. "At the risk of butchering a poetic thought with my country boy ways, I want to make a point about this place. After living away for over a decade now, I can say that the lonely, mysterious river, woods, and marsh are like magic that gets in your blood. I can't explain it with the right words. It fills your heart and your mind."

Quincy remarked Mercedes said something like that to him when she tried to describe the Lowcountry and the deep patriotic roots it had. "Being here, immersed in the Lowcountry landscape, learning about the history and varied cultures that lived in this place—I think it's becoming a part of me, too."

They paused at the entrance to the back cellar, catching their breath. Mercedes looked up the photo of the only Bible verse they had not explored. "Okay, treasure hunters, here's your last clue. *But he answered and said, It is written, Man shall not live by bread alone, but by every word that proceedeth out of the mouth of God.* Matthew 4:4."

Jana said, "I think the keys are 'bread' and the word of God—a Bible or accounts of things that happened in it."

The cellars were cool after the hot summer sun, and though shaded, there was abundant daylight from the beautiful cathedral arches that supported the front portico. Wallace pointed out a jagged crack in the English brickwork on one wall, but it was the only visible damage from the earthquake of 1886. The ceilings were about seven feet high, but they were uncertain how deep the decades of dirt and silt were on the floor. Several large hooks hung from the beams overhead.

Items stored there were dry, and plenty of boxes, crates, and chests hinted at contents kept for future use or to reveal a story of the past. "I don't know when I'll have time to go through these," Wallace said, waving a hand. "My uncle tried to keep things cleaned out, but he kept tools we could use around here. He kept things that were specially made for the house ever since it was built, like old brass hardware, slates for the roof, stuff like that. That's why that key to the padlock on that metal box was still around."

Walking through the cellars was like a tour of the walls in a blacksmith or a hardware store. But near the entrance on the side where the detached kitchen building was, a large wall area was blank except for a sculpted depiction of Leonardo da Vinci's painting of *The Last Supper*.

Mercedes walked up to inspect the artwork where it attached to the whitewashed brick. She guessed it was marble. "Do you know if this is where a table stood, for the workers, close to the kitchen?"

Wallace leafed through several pages of notes. He found nothing specific to the location, but said they fed workers near the kitchen, and he thought it was reasonable that baked goods would be placed in the shelter of the cellars to cool.

The artwork was the best clue they could have hoped for to show a place where bread was available on the plantation, as well as a depiction of one of the most important events in Scripture. They started exploring the walls, floors, and other surroundings for a hint about where the antique Delft tiles might be. They even investigated the wall and ground outside, where the shadows stretched longer as the day faded. In the end, the best place seemed to be to dig in the years of dirt under the *Last Supper* sculpture.

All three men took a shovel and a section. Mercedes and Jana pushed wheelbarrows of dirt from their work away. They uncovered the original slate floor but found no containers of the valuable tiles.

Wallace wiped sweat from his forehead and adjusted his ball cap. "Pull up the slates," he said.

Carefully, the men started prying up the slate tiles from the ground, stacking them in organized rows so they could replace them to fit. Soon, they uncovered a metal plate. Two of them lifted it off the ground, and Wallace shouted for joy. "There's a hole, and a few crates stored in here!"

He turned to find a crowbar among the tools hanging on the walls of the cellar, and Zeke and Quincy started puzzling over how to lift the crates out. "We should open and unload them, then just pull them up," Quincy said. "They're old enough to break apart with the stress, destroying whatever they contain. If this is where the extra tiles are, that would be a tragedy."

With the crowbar, Wallace carefully pried one crate open. In the pink, pearly light of a coming sunset, he took out the first treasure of their last clue. It was a white Delft tile painted to show Christ breaking a loaf of bread over a basket containing a fish.

Declan came out of a long, steaming, relaxing shower that made him smell like fresh cut cedar. He and Zach had watched an adventure movie, then Zach took the first shower while Declan caught up on email. They planned to spend the evening with video games, pizza, and whatever the hotel would put out for dessert down in the hotel lobby.

But Zach was not in the room. The hotel stationary notepad and pen were on Declan's bed with a message. *Order pizza. Don't wait on me, I just got a message and need to go out for a while. See you later.*

It was not the wording of Wallace's message that made Mercedes pause. There was nothing fishy about it.

She looked up from her phone at her brother, her boyfriend, and her friend Jana. Everyone was excited but worn out from digging and exploring in the humidity of a Charleston summer day. A coming storm would give the Lowcountry flora and fauna a refreshing drink, and they hoped to outrun it on the way home.

Tomorrow, they would unpack the rest of the Delft tile from the crates in the cellar. Heady with their astounding success, Wallace promised Mercedes she and Jana could explore the Freedom Staircase in the house to see if she could find any clues about its patriotic name.

As her group packed up the back of the Jeep with the equipment they used, they chattered about whether they were too ravenous to wait for a meal at the Ellison family house and where to stop for something on the way. Mercedes said, "Hey, I need to run to the house for a minute. Wallace just sent a text asking if I will come back to get a gift the housekeeper left for me."

They looked surprised, and Zeke wondered aloud if she made more of the fruit salad she served at lunch. He was crazy about it and asked her to give the recipe to Mercedes. He and Quincy continued to work to make a box fit in the trunk.

Jana peered into her friend's face, lit by the bulb in the Jeep and solar lights in the parking area. "I'm going with you," she said. "Grab a flashlight."

Quincy glanced up. "Here, take this one. Try not to get stuck in a conversation, ladies. There's a storm on the way."

Night settled softly on the plantation, streaking the sky with a last light over ominous looking stormy clouds. Thunder rumbled in the distance. As Mercedes and Jana kept flashlights on the steppingstones laid in oyster shell gravel, Mercedes noticed the windows of the mansion were black. She wondered aloud why Wallace had not turned on any lights.

But he left the cheerful back porch light on, and they climbed the steps. The main door was open, with only the screen against the nocturnal insects and wildlife. Mercedes knocked and called Wallace's name. When there was no answer, Jana said, "He knows we're coming, so maybe he went to have his shower. He left the light on, and the door opened for us. The housekeeper probably put the gift in the kitchen or dining room."

"Yeah, he's expecting us. I think it's okay to go on in."

The screen door hinges wanted oil, and the darkness amplified the squawking friction on the rusty metal. Their flashlights flung stark shadows that jerked drunkenly over the room, and they searched the clean countertops and table for something the housekeeper left.

There was nothing, and Mercedes hesitated. She reached for the switch on a small lamp near the hallway leading to the dining room and found the bulb gone. Jana urged her into the dining room to check the big formal table, and a Styrofoam cooler sat on it with a note.

Relieved, Jana handed her the message while she put down her flashlight and opened the cooler. Out loud, Mercedes read, "There are no thanks that can ever be enough for what your group has so selflessly done for Majestic Oaks and my dear friend, Wallace. This is a small token of my personal thanks. You'll find the secret plantation recipe for the fruit salad at the bottom of this. May the Lord bless you to enjoy it as long as life lasts, but please keep it private within your own families."

"Oh, Mercedes, she put the salad in a beautiful blue willow bowl that looks like an antique! And she surrounded it with ice packs, so it should be fine until we get home."

Mercedes started at a scuffling noise behind her. Wide-eyed, Jana quickly replaced the lid on the cooler and hissed, "Mice? Let's get out of here."

But they froze. On the other side of the room, a mahogany door swollen with humidity opened with no one to shut it, creaking for what seemed like an eternity. Mercedes and Jana swung around to look at it, ready to face they knew not what. "Mercedes, do you feel it?" Jana whispered.

Thunder from the rainless storm rumbled over the river. Mercedes shivered, put the housekeeper's note down on the polished wood table, and touched the silver dagger sheathed in her pocket. "Yes. You shouldn't be with me—I should have known better than to bring you here tonight."

Jana came close, rubbing the gooseflesh on her arms. "Don't say that. Where's Wallace?"

"If he could respond, he would greet us," Mercedes whispered close to her ear. "I sensed something was off when I got his text."

They peered through the distorted shadows in the dining room to the staircase and front door. Shoulder to shoulder, they inched toward the back way out, as they had arrived, and to be closer to running to Zeke and Quincy. But they stiffened at the sound of a voice in the blackness.

"You can't escape this time. I'll get you both and this will be over."

Mercedes never knew in times like these where her resolve came from, but she suddenly became energized and bold. "My friend has nothing to do with this."

A maniacal laugh erupted from a place not visible in the dark house. Unnerved, Jana grabbed Mercedes' arm and groaned. "Let's get out of here!"

"But Zach Boone has plenty to do with it. She can be the witness to how I took care of you both, for my father."

Mercedes whispered into Jana's ear to sneak out and bring Quincy, then she turned back to be a distraction for the disembodied voice in the dark corners.

But another voice, steely and confident, came from the shadows. "I'm the one you want, Roland, but killing me won't satisfy your jealousy. You know the story—your great-grandfather raped my great-grandmother, a socially disgraceful situation for her in those days. Every justice she turned to was on your family's payroll, so she married a friend who sympathized with her desperation when she found herself pregnant. They kept it a secret until your father revealed it to me. You're a liability the partners refused to allow in the firm, and he needed to keep the assets in the family and settle an old score. He tracked me down, but I didn't cooperate. He's gone now, Roland. You can walk away."

"Zach? What are you doing here?" Mercedes exclaimed in dismay.

The terrifying voice laughed again in the blackness. "I lured him here, as I lured you. Such irony! He told me not to hide behind a woman, to meet him in person, so I told him not to run from a woman and meet me here. He thought it was an outdoor event, just us two, but I tricked him at the last minute, and he had to come inside. Not fair, I admit, but I play by my own rules. If he stopped me from getting to you, he won, and you were safe. That was the deal. But I got here first, came in and saw the gift for you in the kitchen. It was perfect, an easy way to get you inside, if I could only silence the homeowner and use his phone."

"Mercedes, go to the stairs and get out of our way." Zach's voice was quiet.

She took a step and hesitated. "But Jana—"

"It'll be over by then."

The laughter of a lunatic reverberated in the walls of the shadowy mansion. She moved reluctantly toward the front stairs while Roland Lenoir's voice rang out. "Wait for me, darling. Zach's first, you're next."

"No!" she cried. "He's your dad's victim, Roland, just like you are! There's no reason to blame him over an old vendetta he was never part of."

"Save your breath," snarled Roland. "This was my father's last wish if he failed. I'm his vengeance."

"He won't listen to reason, Mercedes, we're past that. I tried everything, and he won't go to jail for threats. This will never end until we face him."

"Zach, be careful!" Mercedes pleaded.

"I will. But be ready if he gets past me. Bullets go through walls. Look for a weapon and a shield."

"Jesus, protect him," she prayed under her breath, scanning the room for a weapon before she remembered she had one in her pocket. "What do You want me to do? Please send help!"

Jana stumbled, running through the night, bashing the toe of her tennis shoes on a flagstone, but regaining her balance before falling. Guided by her flashlight, she made it to Zeke and Quincy.

"Quincy!" she cried, out of breath as she came into the clearing. "Lenoir's son is threatening to kill Mercedes and Zach in the house!"

He and Zeke exchanged a shocked look before they checked for their weapons and bolted for the old mansion. Jana followed, shouting, "Be careful! He lured them here, to kill them both."

Two gunshots exploded almost simultaneously as they rushed down the dark path to the back porch, where the light was now off. Jana cried out in dismay, and Quincy burst through the back door. Zeke shouted to Jana to call the police.

Mercedes gripped the balustrade on the staircase railing, watching in horror as Zach and Roland came out of the darkness, silhouettes that faced each other like a showdown in a Western movie. Zach's tone was steely and sure. "Don't make me shoot you."

Time seemed to stop. She held her breath, horrified yet hopeful of divine intervention. Zach had redeemed himself, defending her for the first time since they met. He was an excellent shot, she knew, and in a sliver of light that crossed his face, his eyes held no fear. He waited, feet planted, for his adversary to back off or point a weapon at him.

Roland's arm rose, pointing at his prey. Zach quickly aimed and fired. He jerked backward, but Roland reeled back, too.

She had instinctively covered her ears against the explosion of noise from the gunfire, screaming Zach's name, but put her arms down quickly as he crumpled to the hardwood floors. She heard his head hit hard, and she choked back a sob as she took a step to run to him. But Roland staggered toward her, gasping, blocking her path to his victim. His eyes were wild, dangerous—and certainly not human.

With a flood of recall, she heard Declan's description in her mind of how Zach described this look in Stanley Lenoir's eyes. Was she seeing the same insanity, or the same demon, in his son? Had Zach stared into those same eyes again when he shot Roland?

The back door burst open, and she heard Jana's cry of dismay. Glancing beyond the menacing young man who now stalked her, Mercedes saw Quincy and Zeke come in cautiously, pointing pistols around in looming, angular black shadows of walls and furniture. In the eerie up lit distortions cast by her flashlight on the floor, Jana cradled Zach's head, sobbing, and then she fumbled with her phone.

"Jana is he okay?" she called out with a shaky voice. Roland stepped closer.

"He—he has a pulse," Jana stammered. Her phone was at her ear now.

"Quincy!" Mercedes' voice rasped as she crept backwards. Roland limped to the stairs, eyeing his quarry. "Please, don't get hurt!"

Quincy planted both feet with his gun pointed at Roland. "Let her go, Lenoir," Quincy's confident warning boomed in the house like the thunder outside, followed by blinding lightning that flashed off and on in the dimly lit stairway.

Zeke took a stand on the other side of the staircase, out of Quincy's range. Roland barely glanced at him. He had nowhere to run, but to escape was not his intention. He leered at Mercedes while she backed several stairs up to get away from him. "Stay outta this," he snarled to Quincy, never taking his eyes from her. "They're the reason my father is dead."

"I heard he killed himself," Quincy countered, moving two steps closer and planting his feet again. Mercedes knew he had a deadly aim. All Roland had to do was raise the automatic pistol in his hand and Quincy would face the fact that he took a life. Even though his job was to protect her from Roland, she knew shooting a person would change him.

But Roland must think it was worth it to die killing her. With a derisive laugh and that unhinged look in his eyes that disturbed her so much, he remained at the bottom of the staircase and addressed Quincy. "Men like him don't kill themselves and you know it. He knew things, too many things, too many people in the wrong places. They couldn't let him squeal, so they killed him. You know who I'm talking about."

Mercedes whispered a prayer for help again, desperate that she, her brother, and her friends would be safe. She saw blood spreading on Roland's shirt from Zach's bullet. If she could distract him until he could no longer stand upright, they had a chance.

"Roland, the land will never be mine," she rushed to say, creeping back up another step and clutching the polished mahogany banister. "Even if your dad's plan for Zach and me went into action, it would fail. My father owns it and he's donating it as a park."

Her brother chimed in with an urgent air of authority. "It's the truth, Roland. I'm her older brother. Neither of us can inherit that land. Our father created an equestrian park there, with stables and riding trails."

Roland paused, staring up into the darkness in a way that unnerved Mercedes. She felt a comforting presence beside her on the step and turned to see a man, yet not a man. He stood in an eerie light. And at a movement behind Roland, she turned again and saw another presence, dark and predatory.

It had a voice. A raspy, terrible sound made her tremble and shrink back. "You!" it hissed, pointing at the strange man beside her on the stair. "It was you who left the old cedar chest for her to find. You!"

A powerful, calm voice beside her said, "Yes. It was time for Mercedes to know who she is, time for Roland to decide who he will be, and time for the disputed territory to be called what it is. It belongs to God."

Mercedes winced at a crash of thunder and felt the old boards on the stairs tremble. The mansion rattled, then lightning flashes made her blink several times. When she could focus, she heard the black monster behind Roland urging him to kill her, and she saw him raise his gun a little higher.

Instantly, she pulled the silver dagger out of her pocket. She gripped the sheath and raised it, forming a cross over her heart as she held it at arm's length. "Roland, you have a choice! You don't have to listen to him. Someone can rescue you! Jesus died to set you free from the clutches of darkness. Believe in Him, Roland, and ask Him to be your Savior."

Furious, wild, terrible roars erupted from the black shadow behind her attacker. It stretched up onto the ceiling, grotesque, horrifying. "The dagger!"

Mercedes' confidence surged and she focused on Roland's face instead of the terrifying entity behind him. She shouted. "Roland, listen to me! Look at your shirt, it's covered in blood. Please, I beg you to give your heart to the one who shed His own blood so you could spend eternity with Him. Do it while there's time, Roland. Please!"

The pistol shook in his hand, not higher than his waist and never high enough to shoot her. He stared, fixated on the cross, whose silver gleamed and glowed in her hand, reflecting the light from the man beside her on the stair.

Mercedes heard a creaking board, a footfall, from somewhere nearby. Roland's strength was draining, his face pale, and he finally lowered his arm. He gasped, "The angel beside you proves what you claim. He's been following me, and he came between me and Zach at a restaurant. My sister's praying, and I believe." He dropped the gun and lurched forward as if ripping himself away from the clutches of the menacing blackness, grabbing the banister to stay on his feet. He groaned in pain, and Quincy moved closer, wary.

"I believe," Roland repeated, stronger now. The entity at his back disappeared, vaporized. With a grimace of pain, he raised his eyes to the man he called an angel. "Jesus is the one and only Son of God, who died in my place. I believe in this and want Him to forgive and save me. Tell my sister. Tell her I believe."

He squeezed his eyes shut and almost collapsed as he went to his knees on the bottom stairs. "Jesus, please forgive me and accept me into heaven to live in Your glory forever."

In a horrible instant, Mercedes, Quincy, and Zeke noticed a red dot shining on Roland's heart. A crack that could have been thunder shattered the reverence of the moment, and Roland sank on the stairs.

Zeke laid down his pistol and rushed to him, but a commanding voice came from the dark and froze them all. "Stop, Mr. Ellison! Mr. Holmwood, put down your gun."

Quincy saw the red laser dot was now on his chest. He hesitated, looked up to the shining being on the stairs with Mercedes, then slowly bent with his knees to lay his automatic on the floor.

The voice had a strong British accent and came out of the shadows again. "This is the end of the matter. Roland knew too much about his father's business and his death and should never have used the hidden phone. That's how we tracked him. Out of respect to your family's long and distinguished history in my country, Mr. Holmwood, I'm leaving you with a warning. Stick to working for museums and collectors. This is the last fraud investigation you'll take part in. Don't get a name in those circles."

"I understand." Quincy's voice was calm and firm.

The red light disappeared, and the storm crashed outside. Taking a couple of careful steps through the strobe light effect of the lightning, Mercedes choked back a sob. She reached the foot of the staircase, meeting her brother. Quincy ran over to them, and they laid Roland down to see what they could do.

But his spirit had departed. So had the mysterious man he called an angel.

Jana shouted out that Zach was unconscious. Zeke groped about to find a lamp or light to turn on to check on him. Quincy grabbed Mercedes into a desperate hug, holding on as if she might disappear. Outside, a motorcycle roared to life, and another joined it.

Mercedes' voice choked. "I thought for a moment I was going to lose you! The terrible, glowing red dot was on your chest, just like it was on Roland. Was that who killed Stanley Lenoir and his bodyguards?"

Quincy nodded. "I believe so. I thought Roland was going to shoot you," he said tightly. "Did you see what was behind him, telling him to do it?"

"Yes. Did you see who stood beside me, telling him not to?"

"How could I miss him? Have you seen him before?"

She pulled back to wipe tears from her face. "Perhaps, but never like that, right beside me. He felt familiar, and when I looked at him, I sensed he wanted me to understand there was something special about the stair where we stood."

Quincy scowled. "Are you sure?"

She nodded, and they went to the seventh step on the staircase. Quincy ran his fingers over the wooden joints and pulled up on the lip. It was tight, but it moved in his hands. Then he and Mercedes stared. The hollow box of the stair contained a tattered Bible, some yellowed old documents, something that looked like a ledger, and other items.

Mercedes whispered, "The seventh step! This is the Freedom Staircase." She turned to look at Quincy. "The patriots had to climb up the number of letters in the word 'freedom' and look in the last letter, 'm' for 'message,' hidden under the seventh stair. It's absurdly easy when you know the code."

"Where's Wallace?" asked Quincy, looking around. "He needs to see this."

This made her cry out. "Oh, no! I forgot about him with so much happening! Jana and I assumed he was upstairs having a shower."

"It's okay. We'll go find him." Quincy fitted the tread board back in place.

Outside, flashing lights from emergency vehicles smeared over the watery panes of glass in the windows. It had only been a few minutes since Roland's passing. As she went to kneel by his body and Quincy went to meet first responders, Mercedes looked back up the stairs. "The Freedom Staircase," she mused aloud. "Freedom is what Roland found here, and it's the only freedom that ultimately matters."

Chapter 10

Quincy's credentials and a phone call to the officer he worked with made it easier for Mercedes, Jana, and Zeke to account for their presence in the plantation house and why Roland Lenoir and Zach Boone were shooting victims. Once the police found Wallace Hampton with a bruise on his head, tied and gagged, he told authorities about being ambushed at the back door as soon as he left Mercedes' group. Rubbing his head, he said, "I never saw the cooler with the housekeeper's gift for Mercedes. I would've taken it out to the parking lot to them. I didn't send her the message, but it was clever of my attacker to use my phone to contact her, and to use the truth about the gift on the table as bait. My guess is, if you ask my housekeeper, Maisey, she will say she left the gift in the kitchen. My attacker moved it to the dining room to trap Mercedes deeper in the house."

Quincy groaned and looked at the officers who were interviewing Wallace. "We heard no one in the driveway, since we worked until almost dark in the back, in the cellar. Just knowing they were here, hidden and waiting, makes me a failure. I was guarding Mercedes in case Roland came around."

Jana and Mercedes stayed with Zach until they put him in an ambulance. Mercedes whispered to him several times, squeezing his hand. "Please, Zach, be okay! Thank you for trying to stop Roland before he could get to me."

Her brother Zeke assured them it was not the gunshot wound that was serious, it was the way he hit his head when he fell. Declan was on his way and would pick Jana up to join him at the hospital until Zach's parents arrived.

Mercedes blinked back tears and sniffed. "I'll have to remain here with Wallace," she said. "His wife is on her way. Please keep me informed about Zach's status."

Zeke called his parents to give them the basics about the incident at the plantation and that they would be late getting home because they were staying with Wallace, who refused to go to the hospital to get his bump on the head checked out until his wife arrived. Quincy and Zeke tried to explain to him briefly why this scene had played out in his house, answering his questions from the gaps he had in the discussions with the police.

Mercedes could not sit and think or stop to imagine all the ways her ordeal could have gone wrong. Wallace was an innocent victim in a scheme that involved her, and she wanted to be helpful. So, she busied herself by putting the housekeeper's gift of fruit salad into the fridge and raiding the kitchen to make all of them something quick to eat. No one had dinner, so after a poignant blessing, they wolfed down sandwiches and salad.

Wallace shook his head and swallowed. "I told you today I wanted a dog. I should go look for one tomorrow, an outdoor dog that won't ruin the old floors and chew up the antiques in here. A dog would've barked and let us know someone was in the driveway and the house."

Mercedes smiled and said, "Does all this change our plan for tomorrow? Because I want to tell you about the Freedom Staircase."

A blank look crossed his face. "I promised you could look around it. We'll set a time."

She exchanged a look with Quincy, then said, "We can take a break tomorrow for everyone to recover from this attack. I just thought you should know something good came of all this. Quincy and I know the code for the Freedom Staircase and want you to be the one to investigate the contents in the stair."

Still confused, he said nothing. Quincy stood and reached out a hand for Mercedes. "He finished his sandwich. Let's show him. It has to be seen to be believed."

They all walked through the hallway to the well-worn stairs, pausing on the landing to consider it was where Roland's life ended. Someone had taken away the rug, and the blood was wiped up.

Mercedes and Quincy joined hands and took six steps up, saying one letter in the word *freedom* for each step until they came to the seventh one. Mercedes pointed to it and said, "M."

Kneeling, Quincy worked to get the board pulled up. Then they went back to the landing. Mercedes handed Wallace a pair of vinyl food prep gloves she found in the kitchen and told him and Zeke to go look.

When Wallace saw the items tucked away, he sat back, dumbfounded. He had to calm down before pulling on the gloves. Mercedes flipped on another light switch for the chandelier overhead, and he took a photo before disturbing anything in the hiding place.

"How did you figure it out? Did you find another clue?" he murmured, touching the Bible gently, prodding it as if to see if it was real.

"I'm not sure you'll believe this, Wallace, but the mysterious man who stood beside me on that same step wanted me to look there. He didn't say it in words. I just knew. Then Quincy helped me look."

"At least three other people saw this man you speak of, and your testimony about my attacker seeing him makes four. I don't pretend to understand, but I believe you." He sniffed, and with a shaky laugh, he added, "But I'm pretty sure the police don't."

They grinned, remembering the look on the faces of the officers. Then they waited while he explored the patriot treasure hidden in the Freedom Staircase.

"He found a small Bible with notes and names tucked into it," Zeke told his parents and grandparents when they arrived home. Though it was two o'clock in the morning, the Ellisons all stayed up to hear what happened at the plantation. Declan left Jana there earlier, and she filled them in on the attack while waiting.

Zeke said, "There was a small book with names in it, and a list of people who would come through for messages. Wallace recognized some as family names who still live in the area. But we don't know yet why the items remained after the war was over. The owner may not have been told where the hiding place was, for his own safety, and couldn't recover anything when patriots stopped showing up for a meal at odd times."

Mercedes' eyes looked swollen and red-rimmed from crying on the way home. She was emotionally and physically exhausted, slow to reach for her phone when it alerted her to a message. Bleary-eyed, she blinked several times to read it. It was Wallace's wife, using his phone, saying the doctor told him he would be fine after resting for a couple of days. He was being released from an urgent care center, and they would be in touch later.

Relieved at the news, she thought she could sleep, and told her family she would need to rest before she could talk about what happened. Quincy assured everyone he was fine to go back to the guest cottage, and he gave Mercedes a reassuring hug and whispered, "Keep your phone on and by your bed. If you need me, call."

It would be a day off from work at Majestic Oaks. Wallace was doing fine, according to a morning text from his wife, but she was cautious and made him rest. She already had professional cleaners coming in to remove all traces of the assault in the house, as well as get deep cleaning done to prepare for her family to move in. Mercedes smiled to think of such a capable woman embracing her husband's dream and setting the stage to thrive on the plantation.

After sleeping in until ten, Mercedes showered and padded to the kitchen for something to eat. Hot tea and juice set out on the counter, as well as brunch items. She took something for a headache, still recovering from her stress and tears from the night before.

They threatened to come over her again when she prayed for Zach. She caressed the warm comfort of her teacup, took a sip, and looked out at the serenity of the marsh.

The house was quiet. Mercedes wondered if Jana was awake, and what Quincy was doing. Her brother would return to work at the hospital tomorrow, and she knew Jana and Declan would likely return home, too.

She thought of the silver dagger, and suddenly remembered what Roland asked of her. He wanted his sister to know he believed in and surrendered to Jesus before he died. Perhaps the police would contact her if Mercedes asked them to.

Heading to the library, her grandfather's study, she walked in to find him there. His chair faced a picture window, and his Bible was in his lap. Lost in thought, he did not hear her enter, so she went to look out at the view with him. "Good morning," she said. "Or is it afternoon? I forgot to look."

He smiled and greeted her. "Ah, yes. Time. I wonder if it's not like that song, asking if anybody really knows what time it is, or if they care."

Mercedes laughed. "You've always been a cool grandpa. Few can reference old pop song lyrics."

She grasped his hand when he reached out. He sighed and said, "I can't let my mind wonder what might have happened if I hadn't given you Claire's silver dagger. It ages me every time we come close to losing you, child."

Mercedes kneeled beside her grandfather's chair and looked him in the eye. "There's no reason to wonder. It's past. I prayed for help, and Jesus sent a helper. Maybe it was the same helper that stood with Claire when she took her last breath with the dagger in her hand. Witnesses saw him then, and they could see him last night as he stood by me. I can't explain why, but he was no stranger. The authorities may believe we all imagined it, but the people who matter in my life know the truth. At least we're safe from it being mentioned in the news."

He smiled, closed his eyes, and drew a deep breath. In a few moments, he said, "We can never quite describe him, can we?"

She squeezed his hand. "You've seen him, too?"

Her grandfather opened his eyes. "Oh, yes."

They turned to see Mercedes' parents come in, looking for her. Her grandfather said, "Tell her, Dawson, why you believe her story about the messenger last night."

Looking at Mercedes and perching on the edge of the desk, her father said, "Because I've seen him. Someday, I'll tell you about it."

Mercedes rose and her mother came to hug her. "He acted like a messenger, for Roland, and for the entity that tried to control him," Mercedes said. "The grotesque dark thing accused him of giving me the old cedar chest, and the man told him it was time for me to know who I am, time for Roland to decide who he will be, and time for the disputed territory to be called what it is. He said it belongs to God."

Her grandmother peeked around the corner of the open door. Seeing them gathered, she came in.

Mercedes' father said, "I can speak for the message about the fate of the disputed territory. As you know from Scripture, entities are given territories to influence or 'rule' on this cursed earth until the Lord returns. Perhaps the land the Lenoir family owned was part of territory ruled by an evil power. I can't say. But that land was and still is dedicated to God because our family did so when it came to us, fair and square. We belong to Christ, because of what He did on the cross, and all we have belongs to Him. While we owned the land, we sought His will about how to manage it. So, once and for all, Roland heard the Lord's view of the ownership status of the disputed territory."

"Maybe that's why he stopped fighting about it," said Mercedes' mom. "I'm so in awe of how this came full circle. Claire tried to appeal to the first Roland back in 1900 about his salvation on that awful night when he shot her. He refused. His descendant, named for him, came after you, and like Claire, you appealed to him with the same goal. You used the same dagger, but in a different way, a way unique to your personality and situation. And this time, history came full circle."

Mercedes nodded. "Roland said his sister was praying. He seemed to know, to feel her influence. He said to tell her what happened."

Her father said, "You should. If she has been notified of his death, she is suffering right now. See if Quincy or the police can put you in touch with her or give her a message."

Her grandmother said, "Roland decided who he would be, at the very threshold of heaven. The land is no longer disputed. The messenger said it was time for you to know who you are. Is that something you learned last night?"

All eyes were on Mercedes, and she took a deep breath before answering. "It's always been a concern for me, how different my family is from most. Few people think, talk, or act like us, and most don't live with so many unusual things, sometimes scary things, like last night—happening to them. While I had Quincy in my life, I could live that way. But when we went separate ways, I couldn't see how another man would ever understand how different my life might be. So, I acted as if I was in charge and could walk my road, still as a believer, but avoiding anything uncomfortable and supernatural. I chose what I assumed was a boring career, and it's been anything but that. A normal guy came into my life, and I expected a lawyer to be a solid, boring but dependable man to plan a future with. He was an unwitting tool used against me by a long-time enemy of my family, my enemy's relative, and both of us became trapped in an old vendetta."

Mercedes brought up a hand to cover her trembling lips. She squeezed her eyes shut, then opened them and sniffed. "And now, he's lying in a hospital bed, all because I chased a boring life. My way isn't better than God's way, and I'm not running from His will anymore. If that's proof that I know who I am, then it's true."

Jana and Declan walked down the boardwalk of the Ellison family's pier. Quincy and Mercedes sat at the end, enjoying a quiet evening, rocking in the ripples of the wake made by passing boats.

"Your mom sent these," Jana said, handing them two cans of orange flavored sparkling water. Then she and Declan popped their cans open and sat down beside their friends.

"How is Zach?" asked Quincy.

Declan said, "Improving. Mercedes' brother was right, he'll get over the superficial gunshot wound. He's conscious, but they keep him quiet, so he's sleeping a lot. It's hard to draw any conclusions until the swelling on his head goes down, but they are optimistic he'll make a full recovery."

"He woke up a few minutes when we went in, and he asked if you were okay," added Jana. "We told him you were physically fine but emotionally shaken, and he could hear the entire story when he's doing better. He knows Roland is dead by the bullet of the man who killed his father, but we don't know how he found out." Then she sighed. "We'll be the ones to update you about his condition."

"Yes, I know. His parents told the police to tell me not to call to check on him."

Jana leaned sideways and hugged her. "Pray for Jesus to open their hearts," she said. It's not your fault their world was turned upside down by Zach's DNA report and his link to your past. They dislike me, too, for being your friend. They tolerate me because of Declan and because I stayed with Zach and called for paramedics."

Declan took a sip from his water, then watched a sailboat as it seemed to float soundlessly by them. "I checked myself and Zach out of our hotel and have a room just up the road tonight. We leave early tomorrow, so if you don't mind some company, we'll hang out."

Quincy was quick to ask them to stay. He put his arm around Mercedes and said, "Mercedes is feeling a little down tonight. She told the authorities about what Roland told her to tell his sister, but she's not sure the message will get to her. Unless his sister wants to reach out, Mercedes can't get her contact information."

"Oh," said Jana, dejected. After a few moments, she said, "You know, I don't think they will keep something so personal and remarkable from his sister. She will hear of it, even if it's from the angel man who was there. Once, it seemed to me Roland was looking at him when he said to tell his sister."

Mercedes smiled sadly. "Yes, Roland did that. All that matters is that she knows, somehow. It will comfort her."

Declan cleared his throat. "If it's all right to change the subject, that's a beautiful sunset out there, and it seems like the perfect time to say we have something remarkable of our own to tell you two."

Jana beamed at him, then he took a small box from his pocket. "Jana picked this out downtown a while ago, after telling me over dinner that she'd marry me. She wanted to wait to put it on when we were here, watching the sunset."

He opened the box and carefully put a diamond solitaire on Jana's finger. Mercedes pulled Jana to her feet to hug her while Quincy pumped Declan's hand in enthusiastic congratulations. "Does this mean you got the job?" he asked.

"It means I got the job, and we're going to be moving to the area," Declan confirmed. Happily, they sat back down on the pier boards, still warm from a summer day, now splashed in the glow of sunlight that tucked itself in on the horizon. Jana's ring sparkled with the last colors of the day.

Mercedes smiled as she turned the key on the sunflower charm chain and entered her cottage in Bluffton. She put down a bag of groceries on the counter. It was still summer, and she had things she wanted to do, like biking, hiking, kayaking, and being lazy on the beach. She could have done these things at home in Charleston, of course, but there was often too much work to do there. The job at the plantation had taken up far more time than she imagined, and the tragedy that occurred was still fresh enough to overshadow all the joy of the discoveries they made. Wallace would update her on the work a historian was doing for him.

There were two of her prayers being answered the way she hoped. Zach was now recovering well, and Roland Lenoir's half-sister sent her a pleasant message of thanks for telling her about what happened with his faith on the Freedom Staircase.

She went to get another bag of groceries from her Jeep and met her landlady, Lois, coming out to sweep her back porch. "Here, let me help you," Lois said, and Mercedes handed her the bag while she turned to get the last one.

"Oh, Lois, it's good to be back," Mercedes said. "I love going home, but a lot happened, and I need a few days to relax."

"You've come to the right place for that," Lois assured her. "It's too hot outside now to do much during the day."

A playful tap on the doorframe made them turn to see Quincy leaning on it. He grinned as he greeted Lois. "Where were you when I carried her suitcases in earlier this afternoon? I'm the one who needed your help!"

She laughed and said she was running errands, staying in air-conditioned stores. After they accepted an invitation to grill for dinner with her the next evening, Lois went out to finish sweeping the porch.

"I came to see if you'll ride bikes out to Alljoy Beach again, since it's so close," Quincy said. "It's a change, being back in our own places. I got spoiled in Charleston, spending time with you whenever I wanted. Now, we're back to meeting in doorways, outside, with chaperones, and in public. I'm already stressed out about the situation."

Mercedes smiled sweetly and came to adjust the collar of his polo shirt. He made a low growling sound at her touch on his neck. "We're going to relax and enjoy the rest of the summer, remember?" she said calmly. "We have a lot of fun things left to do. Brad needs me sometimes about the restorations at the Popplewell place in Savannah, but otherwise, I'm taking a few days off to clear my mind and get some rest."

Quincy rolled his eyes. "If you're needed in Savannah, let me know so I can arrange my schedule to ride along. I'm not leaving you alone with Mr. Power by the Hour."

Her eyes grew serious. "Quincy, you're being careful what contracts you accept, right?"

He sighed and glanced around, then left the door partially open and took her past the counter to the kitchen. He closed their phones inside her fridge and turned on the water in the sink. Then he looked into her eyes before whispering in her ear. "Of course, I am. I have no desire or intention of becoming an investigator. And I know what you're thinking—yes, I have met the guy before, and so have you, on a dig site. He knew I would recognize his voice, and it would give his message more weight. The sole reason I took that job when they asked me is because of the link to your family, and he knows it. He couldn't leave the plantation with Roland alive, and Roland gave me no reason to shoot. It's over, as he said. My work now is strictly in collections and advising dig site research. I'll also start back up with blogging and teaching. I've hired a designer to set up a new website and you're my first guest. We'll begin with work on the plantation, then see what we can do with the Civil War discoveries in the basement at the Popplewell's house."

She nodded and smiled. He turned off the running water. "So, our phones are nice and chilly now. Want to put them in our pockets and ride bikes?"

"It's the simple things that make me happiest," Mercedes mused, lying back on an oversized beach towel she had stuffed into her bike basket. With a deep sigh of contentment, she gazed through her sunglasses into blue skies and the changing shapes of airy clouds. "There's no reason to rush, no better view and no better place to be."

Beside her on the sandy strip of beach along the May River, Quincy relaxed on another towel. "Then we need to look for more simple things in life. I'm happy when you're happy."

She chuckled. "That's sweet, Quincy."

He guffawed. "That's me, simple and sweet."

Mercedes rolled onto her side to face him. She reached out to smooth back a lock of dark hair from under his sunglasses. "You're sweet, and you have a way of simplifying complex things. You're tall, dark, and handsome, the quiet type until someone needs to know anything. Then, you're brilliant."

Quincy turned to look at her, brows raised in surprise. "Should I be wary of a set-up coming my way?"

She lay back again on her towel, laughing. "Add British wit and cleverness to that long list of attributes."

"What about my British accent? Lots of women find that attractive. And I walk prissy dogs for disabled senior citizens."

"Yes, there's that. You also aid dolphins in rescuing drugged women from drowning in the ocean, you discover long-lost family heirlooms, and you drive a stunning convertible luxury sports car."

Now, he rose to his side, propping up on an elbow to look at her. "If I'm all that, why am I still single?"

She smiled smugly. "Because you've never asked a lady to marry you."

"Will you marry me?"

Mercedes caught her breath, then sat up. "Quincy don't tease me. This isn't something I can joke around about."

He sat up and reached over to take her hand. "Me, either. I need to know, from your heart, if you will spend the rest of your life with me, as my wife, for better or worse, because all those good things you said about me could take a turn for the worse."

Mercedes' hand flew to her lips, and she squeezed her eyes shut, trying to grasp whether Quincy was proposing to her. She opened them as he put a sparkling engagement ring on the finger of the hand he still held. "I've loved you for as long as I can remember, Mercedes Annalee Ellison," Quincy said softly. "I'm asking you to marry me on the quaint little beach where you said the name Alljoy was fitting because you renewed your promise that you would love me, too. Let's go through life together, enjoying the simple things, and when we're challenged by the complicated things, let's count it *all joy*."

Mercedes rose and pulled his hand with her. The May River lapped lazily on oyster shells scattered along the sandy edge, and a soft breeze rattled palmetto fronds overhead. Several dolphins played alongside a couple in kayaks in the river, and barnacles softly snapped, crackled, and popped.

She hugged him, and when he wrapped his arms around her, she whispered in his ear. "I can't remember a time I didn't love you, Quincy, and it will be a happy day when we are finally married."

A teen boy they met before walked by them and did a double take. "Hey, you two lovebirds! Did the photos I took of you turn out okay?"

Quincy kept one arm around Mercedes and reached with the other hand into his pocket for his cellphone. "They were great! Will you take another one for us? It's an evening to remember. She just said she would marry me!"

Did you like this novel? You can continue the adventures of Mercedes Ellison in the Strange Sands Series. Remember to help other readers by sharing your review!

There is a list of **Resources** for readers who enjoyed this novella series and want to investigate certain aspects of it. For Book Clubs, there is a page called **Discussion Topics** to help leaders guide conversations and glean more spiritual insight from the stories. And if you're a romantic, learn more about Alljoy Beach[1] in Bluffton, SC.

Stay updated with me via my fun-packed author newsletter and websites at Southern Sky Publishing[2] and Pamela Poole Fine Art[3], or join me on YouTube[4], Goodreads[5] and BookBub[6].

1.   https://www.locallifesc.com/wayback-lowcountry-alljoy-beach/

2.   http://www.southernskypublishing.com

3.   http://www.pamelapoole.com

4.   https://www.youtube.com/channel/UC9aV3zHRlASXUUBEF7xbT9Q

5.   https://www.goodreads.com/author/show/3934732.Pamela_Poole

6.   https://www.bookbub.com/profile/pamela-poole

Discussion Topics

If you read the first novella in this series, The Old Cedar Chest, what was your impression of the Prologue event? Were there any surprises for you in The Freedom Staircase when Mercedes Ellison's grandparents tell her more about that night, and when she reads aloud to them the journal entry her Great-Great Grand Aunt Mercedes wrote? How does your faith background, or lack of one, contribute to what you think about the encounter between Claire Ellison and Roland Lenoir in the year 1900?

Readers know that there are more dysfunctional relationships around us than positive, healthy ones. Whatever situation we find ourselves in, what can we do to turn things around for ourselves and for others who need to see a good influence? Can we do this on our own, or do we need Jesus to make a way when we can't see the next step?

Like Mercedes in this novella series, have you ever tried to steer your own course in life to avoid living a life surrendered to the destiny Jesus planned for you? How did He bring you back?

How many Bible references in this story did you look up? When I started writing this novella, I did not know what the clues would be for finding the lost treasure at Majestic Oaks. After praying about it and continuing to write, the idea of clues in Scripture just seemed natural. If you have children or grandchildren, maybe it would be fun to make up a treasure hunt using clues from the Bible!

There are many false beliefs Christians embrace about angels, and we should take time to research what's in the Bible. There's enough in Scripture to give us a launching place for our imagination (as I did in this novella series) but it's not a good idea to rely on art from a Christian bookstore to build your assumptions on. Angels are messengers, always sent with a purpose in God's divine plan. They may appear as God's answer to our prayers, but they follow Him, not our pleas or orders. They serve us at His will and they direct worship to Him, never accepting our worship or prayers for themselves.

I've heard remarkable accounts of the ways angels have functioned in the world in missionary settings. And recently, the pastor of a church we attended told the story of his godly aunt's death the previous week and how she told her family about the angels surrounding her. Mostly, it appears we interact with angels "unaware." That leads me to wonder if we could have this experience and only know enough about it to say something remarkable happened, something many people call a "coincidence." I believe there are no coincidences or luck in the life of a born-again believer in Jesus Christ.

If you are in a small group reading this book, perhaps you can share stories you've heard about situations where they acted for the glory of God.

Consider doing a study together on a biblical view of angels.

Resources

Architecture

In the third novella in the series, the main setting is a Lowcountry Plantation in Charleston County, north of Charleston toward Francis Marion National Forest. My descriptions for the mansion and grounds of Majestic Oaks are inspired loosely by a real plantation that readers can visit. I also recommend books by Archibald Rutledge, South Carolina's first Poet Laurate and descendant of the original plantation owners in the early 1700's. I have two, Home by the River and Life's Extras. His descriptions of life at the plantation are informative and poignant. He donated Hampton Plantation and it is now a historic park. Included in the novella is my painting of the Washington Oak from a photo I took there when I visited in 2010.

Hampton Plantation[7]
Home by the River by Archibald Rutledge
(the book that earned him a Nobel Prize Nomination)

---

7. https://south-carolina-plantations.com/charleston/hampton.html

About the Author

Pamela Poole writes inspirational mystery and suspense that explore the intersection of faith, history, and the unseen spiritual realm. Her stories are grounded in a clear Christian worldview and shaped by a deep respect for both historical preservation and biblical truth.

Pamela writes inspirational stories that bring together Christian faith, historic places, and hidden truths. Her novels reveal how the past can press into the present, where faith becomes essential to discernment and courage. Her characters are ordinary people facing extraordinary challenges, learning to trust Jesus when darkness threatens and answers are not easily found.

The Strange Sands Suspense series and the Painter Place Saga blend richly detailed settings with themes of calling, obedience, redemption, and spiritual warfare. Pamela's fiction offers clean, thought-provoking stories designed both to engage the imagination and to encourage the heart. When she isn't writing, Pamela enjoys research, painting in her art studio and on location along the Southern coast and making memories with her family and friends.

The Strange Sands Novella Series

The Old Cedar Chest, Strange Sands Suspense 1
Hilton Head

An antique cedar hope chest.
A hidden panel.
A century-spanning vendetta.

The Old Cedar Chest launches a faith-filled suspense novella series following architectural historian Mercedes Annalee Ellison as she uncovers the unexplainable forces tied to historic properties—and her own family legacy.

Mercedes never expected her great-great-grandaunt's fragile journal and a tattered manila envelope to change her life. Yet the miraculous way they came into her possession—and the unease they stir in her spirit—would give even the most hardened skeptic pause.

Before she can meet her first client or settle into what she hopes will be a quiet summer at a Lowcountry cottage, an ominous shadow stretches across her carefully planned future. Mercedes soon realizes she is the target of a vendetta that goes back more than a century. Time is running out, and survival may mean accepting a calling she never sought and a destiny bound to the legendary Ellison family.

In this heart-pounding Christian suspense novella, Mercedes must rely on more than her education and instincts. Anchored in faith and surrounded by eerie revelations, she learns God equips ordinary people to stand firm against extraordinary challenges. Filled with mystery, history, and spiritual depth, The Old Cedar Chest invites readers to consider how faith, courage, and divine purpose intersect in life's unseen battles.

The Hidden Hallway, Strange Sands Suspense 2
Savannah

An antebellum house.
A hidden hallway.
A tale of passion and revenge.

In *The Hidden Hallway*, architectural historian Mercedes Annalee Ellison faces another assignment that challenges not only her professional expertise but her spiritual resolve.

Tammy and Clayton Popplewell hired Mercedes as they registered and renovated an antebellum house in the beautiful Southern city of Savannah, Georgia. But she knows this is not the boring job she hoped for when she arrives on the first day to find the local police there. What should have been a routine assessment of aging blueprints and structural quirks takes a chilling turn when Mercedes uncovers a concealed hallway that doesn't appear on any original plans.

As Mercedes investigates the history of the property, she must rely not only on her expertise but on God's guidance to discern something hidden—and why it matters now. When neighbors seek her out with a strange Civil War Era tale of passion and revenge, she works to uncover a terrifying darkness and help her clients make the house into the inn where they dream of sharing light—before they give up and she loses the job.

The Hidden Hallway is a gripping Christian inspirational suspense novella blending history, mystery, and spiritual warfare. Set against the rich atmosphere of historic Savannah, it's a story of faith tested, dreams endangered, and the assurance that God is always present—especially where secrets hide.

The Freedom Staircase, Strange Sands Suspense 3
Charleston

An Enduring Lowcountry Plantation.
A Legendary Patriot Refuge.
A Last Stand for Freedom.

It thrilled Mercedes Ellison to be chosen to work as an architectural historian for Majestic Oaks, a plantation that endured and survived wars on American soil. The stately Georgian mansion features the Freedom Staircase, where legendary patriots stopped for refuge in their roles with the Continental Army in the American Revolution. Her client needs help to keep the plantation he inherited, which is steeped in the history of the Lowcountry of South Carolina, home of the Swamp Fox and four signers of the Declaration of Independence.

There are also some unsolved mysteries on the property. Bringing them to light will help her client, and she finds clues in a secret passage used by the patriots. But then her archenemy dies in jail, and his son watches her. The long-standing vendetta against the Ellison family that began in *The Old Cedar Chest* now escalates, and Mercedes knows the danger she faces is real, personal, and relentless. Can she make a last stand for freedom from the past that began with the murder of her ancestor on a stormy night in England?

Blending historical intrigue, Christian faith, and suspense, *The Freedom Staircase* is an inspirational story of legacy, obedience, and the courage to walk the path God sets before us, even when it leads straight through danger.

The Dark Passage, Strange Sands Suspense 4
Bluffton

Faith tested.
Purpose questioned.
Evil revealed.

Mercedes Ellison is hoping for a quiet summer as she plans her wedding—boring clients, simple renovations, no surprises. But the Marlowe House is anything but ordinary.

Doran Marlowe, a former missionary guide, has spent decades traveling the world's most remote regions. His shuttered passageway and unsettling artwork hint at experiences he never fully left behind. His sister Mary Lou, newly returned from the mission field, carries her own burdens —discouragement, doubt, and unanswered questions about her calling.

When a terrifying incident shatters the calm of the historic home, Mercedes finds herself drawn into a mystery that defies logic and explanation. The danger feels personal, spiritual, and disturbingly familiar. In *The Dark Passage*, Pamela Poole weaves a faith-filled suspense story that confronts spiritual darkness with biblical truth. This inspirational mystery asks hard questions about obedience, spiritual authority, and trusting God when the unseen world breaks into the ordinary.

The Devil's Drawer, Strange Sands Suspense 5
Beaufort

An ominous oath taken for personal privilege.
An enigmatic artifact unbound by time and place.
An evil consequence for generations.

A chilling mystery unfolds at Seashell Cottage as architectural historian Mercedes Ellison stumbles upon an ominous black cabinet decorated with ancient Egyptian symbols. Delivered under the cover of darkness, this enigmatic artifact pulls her and her client into a web of secrets that stretches across generations.

As they delve deeper, a private investigator friend joins them in unraveling the sinister connection between the cabinet and a long-buried family oath to a clandestine society. With blood as the ultimate spiritual currency, they must confront the haunting legacy of a deceased ancestor whose evil choices ripple through time, binding Mercedes' client in ways they never imagined.

This gripping story is filled with mystery and revelations. As a Christian, Mercedes knows that Jesus reverses curses. But will her client come to know this before it is too late?

In *The Devil's Drawer,* Pamela Poole weaves a faith-filled suspense story that confronts spiritual darkness with biblical truth. This inspirational mystery asks hard questions about spiritual authority and trusting God when the unseen world breaks into the ordinary.

Grab your copy today and join Mercedes on this thrilling adventure!

New in 2026!

The Black Hourglass, Strange Sands Suspense 6

St. Augustine

In the shadow lies the truth.

A hidden letter.
A stolen fortune.
A secret that refused to stay buried.

Quincy Holmwood thought his work in St. Augustine was over until a cryptic message from a church archivist pulled him back into a mystery from 1688. How can he resist a search for the truth left by a murdered friar about hidden evidence of a crime against the Crown, committed by a powerful group of colonial settlers of America's oldest city? The trail of clues had endured for the courageous man of a future generation who was bold enough to follow them.

With his fiancée, **Mercedes Ellison**, and a small archaeology team, Quincy races to decode symbols tied to a forgotten brotherhood whose emblem—the **black hourglass**—marks the flow of time the brotherhood believed was under their control.

The brotherhood's final heir is watching his progress.

And he never wants the past to come to light.

As accidents turn deadly, Quincy must rely on his faith and the conviction that he is the one the friar believed would someday reveal the truth.

What was hidden in darkness was never meant to stay there.

Other Books by Pamela Poole
<u>Southern Sky Publishing</u>[8]

The Painter Place Saga
Painter Place
Hugo
Jaguar
Landmark

3 Legends of Painter Place (short stories)
The Wind Songs of the Marsh
King's Ransom
The Castaway and the Mermaid

Southern Sky Devotional
Inspired Artistry—Embracing the Creative Calling

---

8. https://www.southernskypublishing.com/